"You, my friend, have hidden talents," Holden whispered

The tone of his voice was warm and promising, like hot fudge sauce as it hits ice cream, making it melt.

"You have no idea."

And suddenly Kimi was aware that she was naked beneath a hotel robe, her skin still damp from the bath.

She could ignore his comment, laugh it off, but she had a feeling she'd only postpone the inevitable. She looked up slowly, let her gaze connect with his. She was beyond delighted with him. It seemed they'd started out on the wrong foot and now they were learning to work together, maybe trust each other. It wasn't such a big step to indulging in a little extracurricular fling.

"What hidden talents?" she asked softly.

Holden reached out, and with one finger followed the path of a damp ringlet from behind her ear, following its path down her neck and to the curve of her breast.

How far would he go? she wondered.

How far would she let him?

Blaze™

Dear Reader,

I love fashion. I love shopping for clothes, getting to know the latest trends, putting an outfit together—and oh, do I love shoes. I also love France. I love the food, the wine, the chateaux along the Loire, the fields of lavender in Provence and, of course, Paris.

So when my editor asked me if I'd like to do a book for LUST IN TRANSLATION, I immediately said, "Put me down for Paris! Can I write about couture week?" Luckily she said *oui!* It's tough to complain about your job when it involves reading fashion magazines, attending fashion shows and, naturally, shopping. I hope you enjoy reading *French Kissing* half as much as I enjoyed writing it. Visit me anytime at www.nancywarren.net

Happy reading,

Nancy Warren

NANCY WARREN
French Kissing

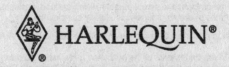

TORONTO • NEW YORK • LONDON
AMSTERDAM • PARIS • SYDNEY • HAMBURG
STOCKHOLM • ATHENS • TOKYO • MILAN • MADRID
PRAGUE • WARSAW • BUDAPEST • AUCKLAND

ISBN-13: 978-0-373-79393-8
ISBN-10:   0-373-79393-6

FRENCH KISSING

ABOUT THE AUTHOR

USA TODAY bestselling author Nancy Warren lives in the Pacific Northwest, where her hobbies include walking her border collie in the rain, antiques and yoga. She's the author of more than thirty novels and novellas for Harlequin Books and has won numerous awards. Visit her at www.nancywarren.net.

Books by Nancy Warren

HARLEQUIN BLAZE
19—LIVE A LITTLE!
47—WHISPER
57—BREATHLESS
85—BY THE BOOK
114—STROKE OF MIDNIGHT
    "Tantalizing"
209—PRIVATE RELATIONS
275—INDULGE

HARLEQUIN SUPERROMANCE
1390—THE TROUBLE
    WITH TWINS

HARLEQUIN NASCAR
SPEED DATING
TURN TWO

With heartfelt thanks to Carol Crenna
for answering all my behind-the-scenes fashion
questions, and to Sharon McKenzie for all the
years of friendship.

1

"I LOVE PARIS in the spri-ing-time" was playing in Kimberley Renton's mind as she headed to her first big event of couture week in her favorite city in the world.

Her over-the-top heels clicked like fingers snapping to the beat of the song as she walked along the Rue de Rivoli. Her designer skirt in black-and-white taffeta pirouetted around her. The matching black jacket frowned down at such exuberance while the crisp white card in her hand gave her entrée to one of the best parties in the fashion world.

As fashion editor for *Uptown,* one of the most respected women's magazines in the States, Kimi was in Paris for couture week to see the greatest clothing designs in the world unveiled for the very first time. She had a front-row seat to every fashionista's fantasy.

She watched as celebrities arrived at the discreet address of Simone, enjoying her reign as *the* top French designer. The tabloids, TV and gossip mags would, of course, showcase the stars and starlets who helped give couture week its sex appeal, but she knew that for this one week, she and her kind were more important to the top designers than that pop singer and her movie-producer boyfriend, now stopping for a photo at the top of the red-carpeted stairs, or the recently reconciled A-list stars emerging from their shiny black limo.

Still, it was fun, in an Academy Awards-night kind of way to watch the hoopla surrounding the celebrities. There were plenty of photojournalists and cameras to document the arrivals. A hundred or so fans and gawkers hung around at the bottom of the steps taking in the show.

As the black limo glided away, a white limousine pulled up. As the door opened, a muffled scream came from the crowd. Nicola Pietra emerged from the limo and paused, so accustomed to being photographed that she had her trademark sexy but rather sad smile on her face even before the folds of her gown had settled. A waiflike young woman with cascading dark curls and dark, slightly slanting eyes, she was an Italian screen goddess with a gorgeous face and body and searing sexuality.

Her accent was slight enough to be pretty and she seemed to cultivate the inevitable comparisons with Sophia Loren and Gina Lollobrigida. Kimi, half-Italian herself, had enjoyed following Nicola's rise to fame, first in Italian art films and then in bit parts in American movies, to her current status as bona fide movie star. The actress's jewels flashed in the glare of the cameras as she waited for Mark Apple, America's Number One Box Office Stud to join her, and then the pair gave the photographers and fans a few moments to snap and gaze their fill.

With efficient bodyguards keeping autograph seekers at bay, they walked slowly up the steps arm in arm. Their approaching wedding was causing a frenzy not seen since TomKat had obsessed the world. Like TomKat, Bennifer, Brangelina and Posh and Becks, this couple also had its cutsie moniker.

Nicola Pietra and Mark Apple had only too easily become

ApplePie. And not a slice would be left after the media were done with the pair, Kimi thought, watching the flashing bulbs, and listening to the questions and good wishes shouted in many languages. It was one of the worst-kept secrets in Hollywood that the pair was in Paris for fittings for the wedding dress for their highly anticipated nuptials.

Even in Paris, a city famous for its disdain of celebrity, there was a crowd out to cheer at the couple. Rumor had it that Mark Apple, whose string of hits seemed to have gone to his pretty head, had tried to rent Buckingham Palace for the wedding. When told he couldn't rent the queen's home, he'd attempted to buy the luxurious palace. He'd been quoted as saying that since he had three times the net worth of the Windsors, he was still willing to negotiate a deal.

Based on the couple's idea of a wedding venue, Kimi could only imagine what the gown was going to be like, and wait—along with the rest of the world—for its official unveiling this week.

Prior to the wedding the gown was to be modeled here at the couture show. That was the condition that Simone had negotiated before agreeing to design the exclusive dress. Simone, as full of whims as the bridal couple, was arguably the greatest designer of the new millennium. Her designs were outrageous, unforgettable, and the cost of a gown was never revealed. It was another of her conditions. She followed the maxim that if you have to ask the price you can't afford it to the ultimate degree.

At last, Mark, in Armani, and Pietra in a stunning Valentino gown of crimson silk with a feathered train, entered the hallowed halls of fashion and, almost immediately, the crowd thinned. In a mixture of French, Italian and English, Kimi heard the verdicts. The English comments were mostly about the couple's looks. He was so much shorter than he looked in the movies, she was too thin.

The French comments concerned the couture. Armani, how obvious. With her chicken-bone frame, the red was *de trop*. But the Italians were more forgiving. Such a body. Have you ever seen such gorgeous hair?

Now that the celebrities had made their entrances, Kimi thought it was safe to follow. As she walked the final few steps to the stairs, she allowed herself one last moment alone with her favorite city.

A glance up Rue de Rivoli showed a tree-lined boulevard so fashionable it couldn't exist anywhere else. Lights twinkled and well-dressed pedestrians enjoyed the crisp evening air. If she tilted her head she could see the Louvre as elegant as a lady holding court. The Seine drifted by, never in a hurry, keeping time, it seemed, with the lovers strolling along its banks.

One of these nights she'd sneak off and enjoy Paris as a tourist, but tonight, she reminded herself, turning back to the fashion house, she had to work.

As she turned and took a step in the opposite direction she nearly collided with possibly the only unfashionable man in the whole street. She caught a glimpse of a tall, rangy build, hair that was thick and shaggy, a tweed coat that had to have belonged to this guy's dad—if not his grandpa—worn over jeans that no designer would ever grace with his or her name.

"I'm sorry," she said, stepping back from a surprisingly solid belly she'd bumped.

"You speak English?"

"Oh. *Oui.* Yes." In the shock of the moment she'd forgotten to speak French and from the pleading note in the stranger's tone, he didn't understand the language anyway. "Can I help you with something?"

He pulled out from an inner pocket a white cardboard rectangle very similar to the one she held in her hand. "I'm looking for number 45."

She blinked. "Why?"

Now it was his turn to show surprise. "There's some party I have to go to. A fashion party."

"A fashion party." Calling Simone's salon a fashion party was like calling the *Mona Lisa* a little picture.

He was looking down at her—and she was a tall woman, so it was an unusual experience—with eyes that twinkled a bit behind intellectual-looking round, steel framed glasses. He was American and if he wasn't out of his element enough being an American in Paris, he'd shown up to fashion week looking like the American male's greatest insult to fashion. And the American male excelled at that activity.

"Yeah. It's for some fashion designer. You look pretty dressed up. I thought you might know about it."

"I do. I'm attending the party myself. It's right there," she said, pointing the way.

He let out a breath. "Thanks. I showed the cabdriver the invitation and he let me out and drove off before showing me which house I wanted."

"I don't want to be rude, but what are you doing here?"

"I'm a photographer for the *Minneapolis Daily Tribune.*"

"I see." She studied him a little more openly. "What happened to Harold Vine?"

"Who?"

How could he be a photographer at the *Daily Tribune* and not know the man who'd been shooting fashion for the paper for five years? "He's the usual fashion photographer for the *Trib*."

"Oh, right. Harold. I don't know. I guess he's sick or something. They called me in at the last minute. I'm free-lance."

On further inspection, his outfit didn't improve. He was wearing a shirt that she dreaded would turn out to be flannel, and his boots looked as though they'd tramped the Himalayas. "You've never done this before, have you?"

"Sure I have," he said, sounding kind of huffy. "I've taken thousands of photographs. Some very difficult to capture, I might add."

"I meant you've never covered couture week, have you?"

"Not in Paris, no," he said, still sounding defensive.

"I think I would have remembered you." In fact, she definitely would have remembered him, not only for his total lack of fashion sense, but also for the steamy expression he got when he looked at her, which had her guessing that he would be in the minority of straight guys here this week.

While she'd been giving him the once over, he'd been doing the same. "Do you live here in Paris?"

She shook her head. "I'd love to, but no. I live in Manhattan."

"Huh. You sound American, but you look European."

"The clothes are French. I'm half-Italian, but born and brought up in New York."

"Lucky New York." And she thought, he might dress like

a color-blind tramp, but there was something smooth and sexy about him.

"Shall we?" He pointed to the red-carpeted stairway.

"You don't have to change or anything first?" she asked, pointing to the small backpack slung over his shoulders.

"That's my camera equipment."

"Right." She shrugged. He wasn't her photographer and if nothing else, he'd add some interest to the evening.

They walked up the red-carpeted steps together and she heard her companion murmur, "Fancy." If he thought red-carpeted stone steps were fancy she couldn't wait to see his reaction to some of the sights he was going to encounter inside.

She presented her invitation and was waved through with a polite, *"Bonsoir, mademoiselle."* Her companion showed his card and began following her inside.

"Un moment, monsieur. S'il vous plaît."

"Huh?"

"He wants you to stop."

He let out a sigh of annoyance. "What are these, the fashion police?"

She smiled. "That's exactly what they are. And if you don't do what they say you'll be thrown out on your American ass."

She listened to the stream of quick French, picking up enough of it to say, "It's your backpack. You can't take it in."

He hauled the pack off his shoulder and unzipped it. "Go ahead and search it. It's camera equipment. I'm a photographer."

"They're French. Not deaf," she reminded him.

The head security guy shook his head and addressed his

comments to her. *"Pas de sacs dans le salon."* He held out an imperious hand.

"You can't take the bag in with you."

The photographer tightened his hold.

Inside, she could see the party was in full swing and she needed to get her butt in there and mingle. Besides, this little drama was getting tedious.

"Hope you work it out," she said, and with a wave, stepped into the sea of couture.

The elegant rooms were crowded, and waiters in formal wear cruised through carrying silver trays packed with flutes of champagne.

Here we go, Kimi thought, sucking in her stomach in one of the few places in the world where a woman five feet eight inches tall and weighing one hundred and thirty pounds could feel fat.

Everyone here, celebrities, models, designers and fashion lovers was beautiful and thin, or rich enough to fake it. The clothing alone was worth millions and the value of the jewels displayed on famous necks, ears, wrists and fingers was beyond her calculation.

She took a breath and caught the mingled scents of expensive perfumes. She loved the glitter and shine, the over-the-top glamour.

Voices spoke in French, Italian, English, Farsi, Japanese and a dozen more languages. She was comfortable in French and Italian, especially here where the conversation remained superficial and about fashion, so she took a glass of champagne that a waiter offered her and stepped forward.

She began working the crowd, greeting the journalists

she knew, the designers' assistants who were invaluable to her and some of the models.

Simone, their hostess, was holding court from a chair that appeared just a little too much like a throne for Kimi's taste. Simone was gaunt and her eyes shadowed. She was wearing one of her own gowns, in black, of course. She never wore color.

She spoke in rapid French, her hands never still. The crowd around her hung on every word. Even Nicola Pietra and Mark Apple were, for once, relegated to the background of the scene. This act was all Simone's.

Realizing she'd never get near the designer, Kimi glanced around the room wondering who else she should talk to, and her eye was drawn to the photographer she'd met outside. He'd made it inside, though his backpack had not.

He stuck out in this crowd like a—like a what? She observed him for a moment and it seemed that he was also observing. There was a vigilance about him. He held a glass of champagne as though that would help him blend in, when it only made him more an outsider. Champagne was clearly not this guy's drink.

His gaze seemed to be absorbing the brightly colored, chattering beautiful people—and then it hit her, the end of her analogy. He looked like a lone wolf who'd slipped into an exotic-bird aviary. There was something predatory and slightly dangerous about him. His fur might be ragged and dull, but she thought, if the mood struck him, he could cut a swath through this crowd, leaving nothing but a few feathers in his wake.

No one was talking to him, and if ever a man was out of his element it was him. She wondered if she should take pity on him and introduce him to a few people when she saw he was being approached by Brewster Peacock.

Uh-oh. In a business notorious for being bitchy, Peacock managed to stand out. His syndicated column was widely read because his wit was so waspishly cruel. He usually targeted the most defenseless: the model returning to her first season after rehab, the passé designer trying to stage a comeback, and former anythings. Peacock lived by the motto that the pen is mightier than the sword—in his case, the computer mightier than the lawsuit—and his column had slashed many a reputation and probably a few delicate psyches into ribbons.

Even though he always treated Kimi like a favored insider, and had actually nominated her as one of the best-dressed women in fashion in his column, she was as wary of him as she would be of a nest of rattlesnakes.

A smart woman would leave tall, dark and badly dressed to the rattler. But, she'd been brought up to consider the less fortunate. Thanks to her mother, she likely knew more about the plight of women in the third world than most women in the third world. The photographer wasn't disadvantaged in any of the ways that always pricked her conscience and had her writing out her monthly donation to several of her favorite charities before she paid her phone bill, but he was clearly disadvantaged in a way that was liable to ruin his career in fashion before he'd snapped his first photo.

She edged her way closer to the odd pair. Brewster's real name was Boris Pushkoski, but his self-chosen nom de plume suited him much better. He tended to go to the extreme ends of fashion and was, in fact, partial to the peacock's colors. Today he wore a royal-blue velvet smoking jacket, a vintage piece from the twenties. Dior, at a guess. His hair was bleached blond and cropped short. He wore flawless two-carat diamonds in his earlobes, and claimed to have started the fashion in men. He probably had.

He was somewhere between forty and fifty, she thought, and suspected he'd look the same for several decades, thanks to a judicious nip here and a tuck there.

She came close enough to hear Brewster say, "And what do you think of the trend to navel-plunging décolletage?"

A tiny pause ensued while she held her breath and considered bolting.

"I don't speak any French," said the photographer.

Without stopping to think, she laughed as though the line was the richest joke she'd heard in months. "I couldn't help overhearing. It's so nice when someone can laugh at our industry. Brewster," she said, leaning forward for the obligatory air kisses, "I've missed you."

"Kimi, *ma petite.*" He turned his deceptively soft-blue eyes her way. "You are as fabulous as ever." He held her away from him, looking her up and down. "And who did you have to sleep with to get that skirt?"

The photographer looked startled and dropped his gaze to her skirt. She smiled sweetly. "My secret."

Brewster cut his gaze to the photographer. "Our friend here also has a secret source for his wardrobe."

"I told you. His sense of humor is reprehensible."

One black eyebrow rose. "You know him?"

What on earth was she doing? Practically throwing away her reputation in the fashion world for some dope who didn't know couture from his elbow patch? She shrugged. "We've met."

She knew she was being mysterious and that Brewster loved nothing more than a mystery. Mostly so he could solve it and tell the world whatever secrets one was attempting to hide.

In a desperate bid to move the conversation away from the scruffy photographer, Kimi said, "Simone is in fine form."

Brewster glanced over his shoulder to where Simone was still gesturing extravagantly, her mouth moving quickly. From here it almost looked as if she was saying her rosary.

"Spilling her words of wisdom to her acolytes. As if she'd ever tell them anything worth hearing. And, darling, have you seen her latest boyfriend? Some mangy Czech who used to play hockey." He fanned himself with a perfectly manicured hand. "Hockey."

"I didn't know she had a new boyfriend. What happened to her husband?"

"Oh, he's off somewhere, trying to look up some anorexic's skirt."

"I see ApplePie's here. Any idea what the dress is like?" she asked.

"Well, I haven't actually seen the dress, of course," he said, looking enormously pleased with himself. "But one hears things."

As horrible as he was, she couldn't help liking him a little. Especially when he always had the best gossip. "What things?"

He glanced around like a conspirator then dropped his voice. "I hear there are two dresses."

"Two dresses?" She whispered too.

Oh, this was going to be good. She could tell from the derisive gleam in his blue eyes. He looked like Elton John about to burst into song. "One for the bride, and a tiny matching gown for the baby of the bride."

Pietra and Apple had a two-year-old child, which was no secret, but the idea of the toddler wearing a matching bridal gown was news indeed. "You are kidding me."

He'd succeeded in shocking her, which of course had been his intention. He smiled. "Wait and see. And now, ta-ta, darlings, I must have a word with Valentino," Brewster said, and strutted away.

She contemplated the man she'd met outside who looked as though he wanted to wipe his brow. "Thanks for rescuing me," he said.

She caught his gaze and held it. "Who are you?"

"I told you. I'm a photographer from the *Minneapolis Daily Tribune.*"

"Cut the crap. You don't know a décolletage from a demi-train. No one would hire you as a fashion photographer."

2

ONE EYEBROW ROSE, but the eyes behind those glasses glanced at her sharply. He pulled out a business card.

She took what seemed to be an authentic *Tribune* business card and read aloud, "Holden MacGreggor, photographer."

"I'm Holden MacGreggor," he said, as though she might think the card wasn't his. She was glad he had the sense not to try to shake hands, since she'd insinuated to Brewster that they already knew each other.

"Kimberley Renton, fashion editor, *Uptown* magazine."

She gazed at the card as though it might tell her more than the skimpy information so far revealed. "Who's your editor?" She knew most people in the business, including the fashion editor at his paper. A woman who'd chew this guy up and spit him out if she saw him show up at a couture event dressed as though he did his clothes shopping at Goodwill.

"Marsha Sampson. I'm supposed to meet her here."

"You've never met your editor?"

He shook his head.

"You meet her looking like that and your first day will be your last," she promised him. Something was off here. Way off.

"I'm a photographer," he said, sounding irritable. "Not a model. Who cares what I wear."

"See, this is how I know you're not really a fashion photographer."

His eyes were hazel, she thought, very attractive. "I'm doing this on a trial basis."

"Who hired you?"

It was his turn to look her over as though trying to decide about something. Finally, while the question hung in the air, he looked at her face, his expression thoughtful. "Rhett Markham hired me."

"The publisher? But—"

He glanced around. "How would you like to get out of here and get a drink somewhere?"

In truth, she'd already made nice to everyone she needed to tonight. She'd planned to hang around a little longer, but there was nothing stopping her from leaving. Curiosity was what had led her to journalism in the first place, and her curiosity was so aroused right now it was going to need a cigarette when this was over.

"Why?"

"I need some help with something and I think you might be the person I'm looking for."

Something sizzled between them when he looked at her, in a way that she hadn't experienced in a while. "Well, it's an original line, I'll give you that."

His grin was slow and sexy and suggested he'd felt the sizzle too. "When I make a move, believe me it won't be subtle. I need your help as a fashion professional. Really, I can't talk about it here."

She was a modern woman with as much native caution

as any woman who spends most of her life in Manhattan. However, she had her cell phone, and her mother had sent her for martial arts training as a teenager, so she felt reasonably safe with this guy. Besides, she had good instincts about people.

"Okay, I suggest we go right now," she said, taking his arm and urging him toward the exit. "That frightening-looking woman with the bright-red hair is your new editor."

He took one look at Marsha Sampson and ducked his head. "Got it."

With as much speed and subtlety as possible, they made their way to the entrance, where he retrieved his backpack, and they went out into the night.

It was cool and quiet after the noise of the party. Second Empire apartment buildings with wrought-iron balconies lined both sides of the street. It even smelled like Paris. Like green trees and good bread.

"Do you know this area?" he asked her.

"Yes. Anywhere near here we're likely to be spotted by someone in the industry." She thought. "But a couple of blocks from here there are brasseries that should be safe."

"Sounds good." He started off with long, loping steps but soon shortened his stride to keep pace with her killer heels.

"How do you walk in those things?"

"They were designed for beauty, not hiking trails," she snapped.

He grinned down at her. "I bet you've never hiked in your life."

She didn't bother answering, but he'd lose that bet. God, when she remembered those miserable summer camps for girls she'd been packed off to as a teenager. Camps intended to build self-esteem and self-reliance. When all she'd wanted was to go to the mall with her friends.

Her poor mother, who'd tried so hard to raise a daughter in her own braless, Birkenstock-wearing image and instead got stuck with a fashion-obsessed girlie girl. What a mismatched pair they were. She had a feeling she got the fashion sense from her father's side. He was an Italian playboy and one of her mother's craziest mistakes. He hadn't been much of a father, but she figured she had him to thank for her current career.

Her mother, a Yale senior at the time she got pregnant, characteristically had refused to marry him, which he, being both Catholic and family oriented, had wanted. However, Evelyn Renton had also demanded that he support the child financially, so Kimi had ended up with a nice trust fund and a father she'd never met. She understood that she was an embarrassment to a high-level businessman with a wife and four children. Her childish ideas of falling into a big, happy, noisy Italian family had died a painful death when it became clear that her father had no intention of ever introducing her to his wife or her half siblings.

She tried to be philosophical about his choices, and as it turned out, the Italian and French she'd studied since high school, in the stubborn belief he'd change his mind, had come in extremely handy in her profession.

She kept up with her father via Google, and liked to believe he followed her career the same way.

"How does this place look?" Holden asked, dragging her out of her memories, as they passed a small bar on a quiet corner.

"Perfect," she said, and they went inside. Normally, she

liked to sit outside and watch the world go by, but she had a feeling that their conversation would be better conducted inside where there was less chance of them being seen together.

Once they were settled and she had a glass of wine in front of her and Holden a beer, he excused himself, but he returned in a few minutes with his cell phone flipped open, as if he was in the middle of a call. "It's Rhett Markham. He wants to talk to you."

She'd assumed he'd gone to the bathroom. Instead he was making a phone call to his publisher?

Who wanted to talk to her?

She took the offered cell phone. "Hello?"

"Kimi? It's Rhett Markham here."

"How are you, Mr. Markham?"

"I'm fine, thank you."

"How's your wife?"

"Fine. Louise is fine too. She misses the newsroom, but she's looking forward to the baby coming next month, of course. I'll tell her you asked after her. Look, there's something going on and you're the perfect person to help out. I've given MacGreggor permission to tell you everything. We're relying on your discretion. You understand?"

This sounded like a bad B movie. "Yeah. You're telling me not to blab." But blab what? "So? What's going on?" She'd recognized Rhett Markham's voice, and if he'd understood she was trying to confirm his identity when she asked about his wife, he'd given her exactly what she needed, since she seemed to be acting as though she were in a B movie too. Trusting no one.

"I've hired MacGreggor to do an important job. Any cooperation you can give him, I'll be grateful for."

She had no idea what he meant. She didn't work for the man, so it wasn't like he was going to make sure she got a bonus, or an extra couple of days of holiday. Oh well, she'd listen to what this Holden MacGreggor had to say, then she'd decide for herself what was going on and whether she should involve herself.

When she finished the call she handed back the cell phone and raised her brows. "Did you call him to check up on me?"

"Yes."

"Okay, enough goofing around. I feel like I'm in a Bond movie. What is all this?"

"You have to keep everything I tell you in confidence."

She rolled her eyes. "I've already figured that out."

"I'm a private investigator. Markham officially hired me, but I'm an independent and unofficial part of an international investigation into a fashion crime ring. We're doing everything we can to keep this completely quiet."

"Keep what quiet?" She was completely intrigued. Not so much a Bond flick, this was turning into a Philip Marlowe detective novel.

"It started a couple of years ago in the spring couture show, which was in the fall, right?"

"Right. Couture shows are always two seasons ahead. Fall for spring."

"A major couture piece went missing from House of Sienna."

She nodded. "I remember that. The dress was listed but never showed up on the runway. The emcee only said it had been pulled from the show." That happened sometimes and for a variety of reasons, most often because the garment had been damaged beyond quick repair.

"The dress was stolen."

Her eyes widened. "But the security is so tight. Are you sure?"

"Yes. It was never found. Seems like every major house has had a gown disappear in the last five years. One outfit is annoying, but won't break the house, and they figured the loss was carelessness or accident. But somebody talked to somebody else and they realized there was a pattern. After that there were a few hush-hush meetings, and a few of the houses decided to do some quiet investigating."

"And you're here to try to find out who allegedly stole, what, one gown a season for five years?"

"No. We have reason to believe there will be another theft. This season. I'm here to prevent the theft and gather evidence against the perps."

"Cool." She'd always loved detective fiction, and, frankly, the man across from her, with his barely touched beer, was more convincing because he looked exactly like the movie and television version of a P.I. Tough-guy gorgeous, inscrutable. Badly dressed. "So you're undercover posing as a photographer." Which would be fine so long as he didn't have to take any pictures.

"I'm a pretty good photographer, by the way," he said, as though he'd read her mind. "It's become a lucrative sideline."

She wrinkled her nose. "I bet. Catching cheating couples going at it on film. Must be a great job."

"I don't do divorce work," he said, sounding mildly offended. Whether about the way she viewed his profession or his camera skills, she wasn't sure. "I photograph wildlife."

"Wildlife. Bears and deer and things? And you think that qualifies you to come to Paris, and shoot super models wearing top couture designs?"

"I capture some of the most elusive and dangerous animals on film. My work may not appear in *Vogue,* but it does appear in *National Geographic, Nature* and *Midwest Outdoors* to name a few."

"Impressive credentials. But you've never worked with fashion models. Do you have any idea how fast models move?"

"Many of my subjects move pretty damn fast. I've been bitten, spit at, stung, clawed and peed on, but I always got my shot."

"Maybe you do have the skills to deal with high-fashion models, after all."

How he and Rhett had thought this was a good idea was beyond her. It was obvious that Rhett was fronting for interests here in Paris. Equally obvious that Holden MacGreggor had no intention of sharing more information with her than he absolutely had to. Of course, she was intrigued. Did they know which house was being targeted? Or was the whole detective thing based on guesswork? He'd been so vague with details, she didn't even know which houses had been victims of theft in the past five years.

Well, fashion week was never boring, but she had a feeling this one was going to be especially memorable.

"What do you want me to do?"

"You're the insider. The one who knows all the players and can help me navigate."

"What were you planning to do if I hadn't come along?"

He scratched his chin. "I thought I'd blend in. Had no idea it was going to be like that."

And of course Rhett wouldn't know either.

"Fact is, my partner was supposed to take this gig. She knows a lot more about fashion than I do."

She glanced up sharply. His partner. Could mean a purely business relationship, or not. Not that it mattered, of course, this was business they were discussing. Serious business, even if he took it somewhat lightly. "But she got called in to testify on a big case we worked on last year—" he shrugged "—so we changed the cover story and here I am."

So the partner was a professional one, which didn't mean the woman and Holden might not also be romantically involved, not that it was any of her business.

She sipped her wine slowly, thinking. Finally, she said, "So, your plan is to pose as a fashion photographer and you hope to blend in."

"Right."

"Are all your clothes like those ones?"

He glanced down at himself as though he'd forgotten what he was wearing. She didn't blame him. She'd have tried to forget too. "Pretty much. Shorts for summer, you know, and different grades of boots depending on the terrain."

Possibly he was making fun of her, she had no idea, but she didn't care. She said, "I hope that you have a fat expense account. If not, I suggest you negotiate one, because, my friend, before you go anywhere near a fashion event in this city with me, you and I are going shopping."

3

"YOU WANT to pick out my clothes?" He looked less than thrilled by the idea. Probably how she'd feel if he demanded she don hiking boots and head into the jungle in search of some wild, rarely photographed mongoose.

And yet, when she took a good look at him, she felt excitement stir. He had a build most guys would kill for, good features, a thick head of hair. He was a ten dressed up like a minus two.

With the right clothes, accessories and haircut, he'd be something.

This shopping expedition, she decided, was going to be fun. At least for her.

His thoughts were obviously bent in the same direction, if less pleasurably. He narrowed his gaze at her, very spaghetti-western gunslinger. "You're not planning to turn me out like that man-tart in blue velvet, are you?"

She narrowed her gaze right back. *If you want my help, you'll do this my way.* "Those are my terms. If you want my help, you'll not only go shopping with me, you'll buy exactly what I tell you to buy."

The eyes hardened, the six-shooter about to be drawn, "I get veto power." His eyes were an amazing color. Hazel with flecks of gold and green, which distracted her for a second.

Focus, she reminded herself. This was work.

"One veto all day."

A look of revulsion crossed his face. "All day? You were planning to spend a whole day shopping?"

"Of course. And we'll be pushing it to get everything done in a single outing."

He shook his head, leaned back and folded his arms across his chest. "Two hours of shopping and five vetoes."

How anyone so disastrously turned out could pique her interest, she had no idea, but this guy was seriously interesting. If annoying. "Do you want my help or not?"

"I hate shopping," he announced, not a big surprise.

She put down her glass of wine with a snap. "Look, if I needed your help to, say, get to the top of Everest—"

He snorted. As if.

She ignored the interruption. "I would take your advice about purchasing gear, clothing, et cetera, because that is your world and you are the expert. It's the same with couture week in Paris. This is my world and I am the expert. We do this my way."

"The difference is that climbing Everest without the proper equipment will get you killed. Even the moderate hike I might agree to take you on can be dangerous without the right gear. Fashion week in Paris is hardly dangerous."

She smiled. "Clearly, you have never been eviscerated in print. If that man-tart, as you call him, Brewster Peacock, takes it into his head to destroy you in his column, you can hang up your camera. You'll never work fashion week again."

"That—that Kewpie doll in pants has that much influence?"

"Oh, yeah. That means the next time you see him, you

not only have to look the part of a legitimate fashion photographer, you have to talk the talk."

"I am a legitimate photographer," he exclaimed.

"I said fashion photographer. If you want to enter this world you have to understand the rules. Did you do any research at all?"

"I read a copy of *Vogue* on the plane." He sounded defensive. As well he should. Even if he'd been handed this assignment at the last minute, there was no excuse for not doing his homework. Obviously, he'd decided fashion was some silly pastime that he could slide into with no effort. He was about to realize his mistake.

"What are the hot colors for fall?" she asked him.

"You have to change colors? Like the leaves?"

Oh, he'd really knocked himself out with that *Vogue*. "Latest fashion trends? Come on. Something must have stuck."

"Mostly I looked at the pictures," he admitted.

"Well, Holden MacGreggor, we're looking not only at a shopping expedition of at least four hours with a maximum of two vetoes, but you're also going to fashion boot camp."

His lips quirked. "Fashion boot camp?"

"Well, boots, shoes, high-end apparel." He looked so horrified that she threw in a reward. "And if you're very good, and do all your homework, we'll also study lingerie."

"And when do we do all this?"

"Get a good night's sleep. You'll need it. We start at 9:00 a.m. tomorrow."

She leaned back, thinking that she really didn't have time for this. The scent of French cigarettes reached her, potent and bitter.

He pointed to her nearly empty glass. "You want another one?"

She shook her head. "Big day tomorrow. Shall we meet in my hotel lobby?"

"Sure." He obviously knew when he was beaten. He rose when she did. "I'll walk you home."

Old-fashioned manners. Nice.

"How come you're not a model?" he asked her when they were back on the sidewalk and headed for her hotel. "You're more beautiful than most of the women that were there tonight."

He didn't seem like the kind of man who gave out random compliments like air kisses, so she turned to him and said, "Thank you. I started out wanting to model, but I didn't grow tall enough for runway, and—I don't know, I realized I'd have more fun and a longer career if I worked behind the scenes. Besides, I wouldn't have to starve myself."

"So you became a fashion writer."

"I have always loved fashion. Even when I was a kid I had extremely definite ideas about what looked good. I drove my mother nuts."

"She's in fashion too?"

She laughed. "Not even close. She teaches women's studies at NYU. I could recite to you word for word her theories about fashion and its role in imprisoning women."

"And yet you chose fashion as a career."

"I see the other side. I see how fashion allows a woman to express herself."

"Really." He seemed intrigued by the idea, though, based on the way he dressed, he and her mother would get along like a couture house on fire.

An elderly man passed them and as she stepped aside to allow him by, her arm bumped Holden's. Warm, strong and dangerously sexy currents flowed between them. He was one of those guys that you just knew would be great in bed. It was in the way he moved, the confidence in his stride, the way he gave her his complete attention when he spoke to her.

"What are you expressing right now?"

"Pardon?" Had he read her thoughts?

"With the outfit you're wearing." He ran his gaze up and down her form in a way that wasn't sexual, but somehow felt that way. "What are you expressing?"

"You tell me. It doesn't work if I have to explain."

She thought he'd refuse her obvious dare, but he didn't. He pushed his glasses up in a way that reminded her of a professor about to launch into a lecture, and said, "Bearing in mind I know nothing about fashion, here's what I see." He eyed her once more, and this time there was no doubt about the expression in his eyes. "I see a grown woman who still likes to play dress-up."

She raised her brows at that but didn't comment.

"I see a woman who knows her own worth and the power of her own beauty."

A tiny shiver of embarrassment fluttered across her belly. She never consciously thought of herself this way. Was it true?

"You hobble yourself in heels like that," he said, pointing with his chin toward her black-and-white Blahniks, "but you must know they make your legs look never ending."

"And the shoes themselves are pretty," she reminded him. God, she loved these shoes.

His grin was sudden and animal. "I may not know fashion from my ass, but I know that you wouldn't dress in anything you didn't think would enhance your appearance."

She laughed. "You've only known me a few hours."

"I call 'em as I see 'em. Your skirt says you're a fun woman with a frivolous side, and the jacket says you can also be serious. Formal when it suits you." His gaze met hers. "And, speaking purely as a man, I'm getting a sense of a woman who is comfortable with her sexuality."

She tilted her head to the side. "You put that last bit in to be provocative."

"Or maybe you're expressing more than you realize."

Before she could sufficiently annihilate him with words, which would of course entail thinking up something sufficiently annihilating to say, he reached over and kissed her lightly on the lips.

Just a brush of his mouth against hers and she felt her legs go to jelly. He pulled away almost immediately, but she felt as though she'd glimpsed something hot and dangerous. She licked her lips, tasted beer. "What was that for?"

"Good night." He gestured behind him. "We're here."

And there was her hotel, as elegant and grand as Cinderella's fairy godmother.

"Good night." She didn't turn to see if he watched her all the way in. She didn't have to. She could feel his gaze on her. That man was going to be a serious distraction.

KIMI WOKE with that wonderful feeling of delights in store. She took a moment to savor the fact that she was staying in a gorgeous room in a luxurious hotel in her favorite city in the world. She stretched against top-quality French bed linens and contemplated her day with Holden MacGreggor.

She pondered him the way Pygmalian might have studied a lump of clay, foreseeing the possibilities. The build, the intriguing eyes, the rugged planes of the face, that thick, thick hair. When she was finished with him, he'd be outstanding in a city of superlatives.

She ordered a breakfast of coffee and croissants and fresh-squeezed orange juice, showered and opened her wardrobe. She'd unpacked the second she got into her room, and her closet was organized exactly the way she liked. Casual clothes here, business attire here, dressy there.

Her shoes were lined up according to outfit, and her lingerie was neatly tucked in paper in several of the drawers. Lingerie was her secret weakness, and while she was here, she intended to replenish her stash.

She flipped on the TV for the news while she dressed and prepared herself for the day. This was a ritual she enjoyed and one which she never rushed. She'd rather get up early than deny herself the hour it took to dress, do her hair and makeup perfectly.

At five to nine, she was downstairs in the lobby.

In her hand was the list she'd made last night of Holden MacGreggor essentials.

This was going to be a very good day.

HOLDEN WOKE bleary eyed and short tempered. He could swear his bed smelled like perfume, which was fine if a sexy woman were sharing it, but when he was on his own, not so much.

He'd stayed up late studying the file on last year's theft.

A dress had simply disappeared. One single dress had caused all this fuss. How could one dress be worth more than most people earned in a lifetime?

Just confirmed his notion that the world got crazier every day and he was better off in the wilderness, where there was a natural order that made sense.

He showered, unzipped his duffel, yanked out a clean shirt, fresh jeans and underwear, dressed swiftly and was out the door within a quarter hour of waking. He tried to grab a coffee to go at the first café he passed, but the snooty Frenchman behind the bar couldn't—or wouldn't—understand him, and he ended up with a little china cup and saucer. He stood there and downed the coffee, which was at least strong and excellent, before returning the china and heading on his way.

He entered the lobby of Kimberley Renton's hotel at precisely nine and looked around for an English-language newspaper, assuming he'd have to wait, but to his surprise, she rose from a lobby armchair, looking fresh and more gorgeous than most of the women he'd seen in that *Vogue* he'd thumbed through on the plane.

She was a class act. He'd assumed when he first saw her last night that she was a native Parisian, but half-Italian made sense. She had lustrous black hair with just enough curl to keep things interesting, skin that hinted toward gold, a full-lipped mouth that had tasted every bit as good as he'd hoped, and then those eyes. Deep blue, a complete surprise. That slam of blue took a man back, made him see her anew.

He liked her height and her long legs. She looked less formal this morning, but no less fashionable. She was wearing a print dress that wrapped around her figure, making him immediately fantasize about undoing the tie and unwrapping her. She had a brownish-colored leather bag hanging from her arm with the name Prada stamped on it, which even he knew was a big designer deal.

He stepped forward with a smile on his face, thinking he might be able to talk her into coffee and pastries in one of the cafés and then use his manly wiles to get all ideas of shopping out of her head. He got closer and his belly turned to stone when he saw that she had a list in her hand. Lists and women, in his experience, were always a bad combination.

She took a good look at him and he could have sworn he saw her shudder and close her eyes for a moment. Then she got over herself.

"Good morning," she said, perky as all hell. "How did you sleep?"

"Like shit."

If anything, his surliness amused her, which didn't lighten his mood. "Try melatonin," she suggested. "It's a cure for jet lag. Ready to go?"

He was ready to go back to bed, or, even better, to call Rhett Markham and tell him to find somebody else. He'd imagined this gig as snapping pictures of gorgeous women for a week, which he was definitely up for, while tracking down a ring of thieves. He'd never in his wildest nightmares imagined he'd endure wardrobe fittings and something called fashion boot camp, which he was pretty sure he wasn't going to enjoy.

However, he needed this woman's help, so he sucked it up and said, "As ready as I'll ever be."

"Excellent. We're heading for the Champs-Élysées. Just a short walk."

He glanced at her feet and noticed she had flat shoes on today. They had intertwining Cs at the front, which no doubt meant something fancy.

God, he hoped CC didn't make men's shoes.

"I think we'll start with the main pieces first. Suits, shirts. Then we'll move on to shoes and casual wear."

It was going to be a very long day.

In spite of her bossiness, there was something about Kimi that appealed to him. She was so polished, and yet touchable somehow. All his life he'd stayed away from women like this, with their perfect hair, flawless makeup and overdeveloped fashion sense. But she wasn't forever fussing over mirrors or excusing herself to go style her eyebrows or something. She seemed like once she was dressed for the day, she didn't give her appearance much of a thought. Interesting.

Oh, high maintenance for sure, and definitely not his type, but he liked her. He hated to admit it, but he liked her style. She wasn't the kind of woman he'd ever see himself with, but she was easy on the eyes. Nothing wrong with that. And, as an accomplice in this job, so long as she could keep her mouth shut, she was ideal.

He still had to shorten his stride, but not so much today with her in flats. In hiking boots, he had a feeling she could keep up to him pretty well.

He shook his head. What was he thinking?

The Champs-Élysées was one of those streets like Fifth Avenue or Rodeo Drive that would never make his list of top destinations. After walking for a while, she turned off the famous street and he found himself on a quieter and even fancier street. Rue du Faubourg Saint-Honoré. There was a parade of names here, mostly discreetly whispered in gold script. No neon signs here. No big Sale signs in the windows.

He half hoped that his guide and fashion cop of the day would be so dazzled by women's clothing stores that she'd forget all about their mission, but he soon found he'd misjudged Kimberley Renton. She might have gazed with sharp longing in a couple of windows, but she never slackened her pace until their destination was reached.

The store she took him into was sleek, black-and-white decor, everything minimalist—including the clothing on display. There was hardly anything here. And luckily for him, nothing in blue velvet.

A sleek balding man, who looked like European royalty, came forward with a polite greeting and then, when he got close, beamed. "Mademoiselle Kimi," he said, putting the accent on the second syllable. So, she went by Kimi.

A quick volley of back-and-forth French followed, and the obligatory double-cheek kissing, and then Kimi switched to English, presumably for his benefit, and explained that they needed to get him some clothes.

After that, they talked about him as though he weren't there. Monsieur will need three suits for the fashion week, a selection of shirts, ties, the evening wear, *bien sur,* and before he quite knew how it had happened, he was standing in front of a triple mirror in a dark suit with some poor minion on his knees making markings to hem his pants.

"Valentino for the formal," Pierre was saying to Kimi, "Armani, of course, and I think Zanetti for the informal. A nice charcoal two-button suit. Can be dressed up with tie and cuff links, but very nice with an open collar. Yes?"

She nodded. Looking him up and down like she was

planning to sketch him from memory. He very much liked having a woman undress him, but he wasn't sure he was as crazy about having one dress him.

"That's a good start." She shot him a mischievous glance. "We need him gorgeous."

"That goes without saying."

Once all the chalk marks were made he was allowed to escape back into the dressing room, where he hauled himself out of the dress shirt and was standing in slacks and an undone Prada belt.

"Are you decent?" Kimi's voice came from the other side of the door.

"Depends who you ask."

With a tsk that said she didn't have time to dawdle, she pushed open the door. When she saw his naked chest she smiled. "Nice," she said, tapping him on the pec. Her palm was soft and cool. "Exactly as I'd hoped."

He could get all puffed up by the compliment, except that she'd said it as impersonally as though he'd been a plastic mannequin she wanted to stick in a store window. But he was flesh and blood and both reacted to her touch. He felt the brush of her skin against his and his blood immediately pumped a little faster. The change room seemed like a very intimate space with the two of them in here and him half-naked. Maybe she caught the direction of his thoughts for she glanced up and their gazes met. He caught the heat of attraction in her eyes and felt the war going on inside her between the bossy fashionista and the warm, exciting woman he knew her to be.

Then she handed him a pair of sweaters, one black and the other a kind of blue with a pattern in it. They were wool and silk, he found when he peeked at the label, soft to the touch.

"Try these on," she said, and disappeared.

Okay, he thought as she exited, so the bossy fashionista had won this round. The sexy woman in her wanted to come out and play. He'd seen it in her eyes. Maybe having a woman dress him had its moments.

Especially if it could lead to her undressing him, which at the moment seemed like a very appealing idea.

4

"FIND HIM SOMETHING to wear out of the store, will you, Pierre?"

"But of course, Kimi."

"What are you planning to do with my clothes?" Holden asked.

"Throw them away. Please."

He'd been measured, pinned, manhandled and dressed. It was time to assert himself. "But those are my favorite jeans."

"You poor misguided man." She sighed. "I'll make you a deal. You can keep the jeans if we throw away the blue sweater."

"What's wrong with the blue sweater?"

"I don't have time to tell you everything that's wrong with that sweater. We're only in Paris for a week."

"That sweater is very warm," he said.

"That's the only thing not wrong with it."

He squinted his eyes at her, playing for time. There was something decidedly flirtatious about the way she returned his gaze. "You are a very bossy woman."

"Darling, if we're ever in a situation together where we're in the wilderness and need to survive on berries, believe me, you can be the boss."

He handed over his sweater to Pierre but spoke to Kimi. "Don't forget I also know which berries are the poison kind."

She turned to Pierre. "Can you wrap up everything but the sweater and deliver them to the hotel with the rest of his things?"

"Of course." He took the sweater and walked into the stockroom as though he were carrying a dead rat. When he returned, he was empty-handed.

When they left the store, Holden was wearing dress slacks in something he thought was called twill. They were gray in color and over them he wore a black-and-white shirt and the black sweater. He still wore his sneakers, but he had a premonition that he wouldn't be wearing them for much longer.

And when their next stop was a shoe store, he knew he'd been right. He didn't bother arguing. So far, he'd actually liked everything she picked out for him and only used one of his vetoes when she tried to explain that a lavender shirt was not the same as pink.

He thought it was outrageous to pay those kinds of prices for clothing, though after seeing how everyone else at that party had been dressed last night, he acknowledged he needed help.

"I only wear comfortable shoes," he warned her as they walked into a shoe store that looked more like a shrine to rare religious artifacts than a storefront for footwear.

"Lucky you."

"Hey, nobody forces you to wear those crazy ice-pick heels."

She shrugged. "We all have our obsessions. You keep your hiking boots. I'll stick to my heels."

"Have you ever even owned a pair of hiking boots, Manhattan? I bet your idea of the wilderness is Coney Island. You're missing out on one of the greatest experiences in the world."

She looked at him, rather amused. "You'd lose your bet. Among other outdoor adventures, I spent a memorable ten days in senior high in a women's-only survival camp. It included a three-day personal wilderness adventure where we got dropped off in the middle of nowhere, Colorado, each in a different spot. For three days and three very long nights, I had to rely on my wits, scavenge for food and hope to hell nothing worse than mosquitoes ate me."

All her friends that summer had gone to dance camps, theater camps. She herself had been accepted to a two-week workshop for budding fashionistas, but her mother had been determined she should balance out her frivolous lifestyle with more serious and presumably useful pursuits. "I know all about camping in the wilderness, my friend, and it is not for me."

She loved the way his eyes flickered gold and green when he smiled down at her. "That camp was work. An ordeal." He shook his head at her. "That's not how you learn to appreciate nature, by gritting your teeth and eating grubs and berries and shivering alone at night. Your folks should be horsewhipped."

"Only my mom. My dad probably wouldn't know me if he tripped over me." She hadn't meant to sound so bitter, so she lightened her tone. "Anyhow, Mom did her best for me. And I bet I can still build a campfire with a bit of broken glass and some dry twigs."

"Going out into nature isn't supposed to be an endurance test. It should be fun."

She shuddered. One of the million mosquito bites she'd got on that awful three-day ordeal had become infected. Unfortunately, it was near her eye. Her eye had swelled shut and she'd needed antibiotics. When she'd started school that fall, her senior year, she'd still had some redness and swelling. She'd felt like a freak. "My idea of camping includes valet parking. And room service."

"There's nothing like watching the sun come up over the water, and you look out and watch eagles soaring, and there's a deer, right there in front of you and you'd swear he was looking at the sunrise just like you are." He had a nice voice, soothing, so she could almost imagine the moment. The two of them snuggled up watching the sunrise.

"It's quiet, so you can hear yourself think and the air is clear enough to breathe. No cell phones, no traffic, no—"

"No indoor plumbing."

He put an arm around her. "One day, when you decide you're ready, you call me and I'll take you."

"You'll take me camping?"

"That's right. I know a little spot I think would convince even you. We'd hike in, spend a couple of days exploring. If we go at the right time, you see orca whales traveling south. You'd like that."

The words *whale watching tour* flashed through her mind, but she understood he was offering her something that was important to him so she kept her snarky comments to herself. "I'll think about it," she said. "But for now, we need to get you some shoes and—I don't suppose you own cuff links?"

"At home in my safe-deposit box I have a pair that belonged to my grandfather." They were gold with pearls on them. And they were staying locked up where Kimi couldn't get her hands—or his cuffs—near them.

She gave him the kind of smile old ladies give little kids before patting their cheeks, and then preceded him into the next store on the Rue de Boredom.

"Oh," she said, "I've also booked you an appointment at my favorite salon for a haircut." She consulted her watch and looked pleased with herself. "We're right on schedule."

"I suppose I'd be wasting my time if I told you I had a haircut a couple weeks ago?"

She smiled at him sunnily. "You're right. You would."

After finding himself the proud owner of brogues, loafers and boots, none of which he could ever imagine wearing once this week was over, they finally escaped.

To the hairdresser.

Where it took a full hour as Kimi and another of her pet Frenchmen discussed his cheekbones, his jaw, even pulled his hair up to check the shape, size and angle of his ears. They were pronounced excellent. He'd have mentioned how he found them useful for hearing, but decided to save his breath for when they started doing stuff to his hair he didn't like.

But, surprisingly, for all the discussion, he ended up looking way more normal than he'd imagined. His hair was shorter, and maybe more shaped, but he hadn't had to fight off dye, or bits draping strategically over one eye, or strange spiky things, all of which he'd seen in the salon.

Once out, he thought his ordeal was over and that he'd been amazingly patient.

"Whew," he said. "I'm ready for lunch. And then a nap."

She laughed at him. "Well, since you've been very good, we'll have lunch sent up to my suite. But we've got a stop to make first."

He liked the sound of lunch in her suite. But something about her businesslike manner suggested his idea of the two of them alone in her Paris hotel suite, and her idea of same, weren't going to gibe.

Sure enough, their next stop was at a huge bookstore that stocked a large selection of books and magazines in every language. Even as he went over to the mag rack to see if they had any outdoor magazines, she was busily filling her arms with one copy of every fashion magazine the place carried, including a couple of French- and Italian-language ones.

He had a very bad idea in the pit of his stomach that she wasn't going to be reading them all herself.

Sure enough, after she'd paid for the booty, they walked back in the sunshine to her hotel.

"I'll order lunch while you get started."

"Get started?"

She emptied one of the bags of magazines onto the table in the living room. "Boot camp."

"No, please," he groaned.

She walked to a fancy desk that could have been used by Napoleon and Josephine and opened the drawer to find a pen and notepad, which she placed beside him.

"Make notes. I want to know the hot designers, what they're known for, the colors for this season and next, and I want you to be able to recognize the models. You'll be expected to know most of them at a glance. If you don't, you'll be revealing yourself as a clueless amateur."

"Okay, okay. I get it."

He grabbed the first magazine on the stack. Flipped it open.

"I DON'T UNDERSTAND how Rhett could send someone who doesn't know the first thing about fashion," she grumbled.

"I know your purse is Prada," he snapped.

"Good. Maybe by the end of the afternoon, you'll recognize my dress and shoes."

It was going to be a very long day.

And night, it turned out when Her Ladyship informed him that she was attending a magazine editors' dinner and he didn't need to bother coming.

"But—"

"Get more room service sent up. I'm serious about this boot camp. You've got to know your stuff or your cover will be blown the first time you have to work with your newspaper editor."

"Okay." He knew she was right, but of all the worlds he'd had to learn in a hurry, this was the one he had the least interest in. "Look, I'll take this stuff back to my hotel and keep working. Besides, I've got some calls to make."

She gave him a suspicious look. "There will be a test."

He rose and stepped up to her, maybe a tad closer than strictly necessary. She raised one eyebrow and sent him a cool, blue challenge.

"Whatever test you have for me," he said, "I promise you I'll pass."

He had the satisfaction of seeing her eyes widen and her breath jerk in sharply, before he turned on his heel, grabbed his homework and left.

5

THE PHONE DRAGGED Holden out of a troubled sleep. He'd been dreaming he was being strangled by a sadistic killer, and the jangling sound of a French telephone with its jarring *brrring, brrring* had him sitting straight up in bed before he realized that he'd been dreaming of himself in a bow tie. A nightmare if there ever was one.

He snatched at the receiver. "Yeah."

"You had yourself reassigned." It was Kimi and she sounded pretty pissed about the results of a couple of the calls he'd made last night.

"I was going to tell you about it myself this morning. How did you find out so fast?"

She ignored his question. "Why did you do it?"

"I thought about it, and me working with you makes sense. You already know who I am and you said you'd help me. This way I don't have to pretend I'm something I'm not, or let that miserable-looking editor get a piece of me."

"Think you're pretty smart, don't you?"

"Above-average intelligence. What are you so pissed about?"

"I don't like being railroaded into things without my permission. I don't like *people*—" she emphasized the word *people* so it had the same connotation she'd give vermin "—going behind my back and messing with my career. And Paris during couture week is my career."

"You said you'd help me."

"Unofficially. But I'm a fashion editor. Not a detective. I have priorities."

"Okay, fair enough." He shoved his hair out of his eyes and wished he'd already had at least one strong cup of coffee inside him before dealing with an irate Kimi. "I didn't even think of getting myself assigned to you until after I got finished studying and started doing some thinking. It was too late to call you by that time."

"You could have waited until morning. Talked to me first in case I had a problem with your brilliant idea."

"I could have, but it all needed to be done fast. Plus, we needed your people onside. So, yeah, sorry I didn't tell you before. I was going to tell you this morning."

"My publisher called me with the news. It means I don't get my own personal handpicked favorite photographer, the one who flies in from Milan specially. He was supposed to meet me here today. They've given him another assignment. Instead I get you." He heard her teeth snap together and was reminded of the time in the backwoods of British Columbia when a cougar had tried to have him for lunch.

"Don't you think solving a major international crime ring is more important than your career?"

"No. I don't."

He tried another tack. "How do you know I'm not a better photographer than your Milan guy?"

"Let me count the ways. One—he's photographed every major fashion event of the last three years. I've never seen you at a single one. Two—he trained under Richard Avedon."

"Wow. Impressive."

"You bet your ass it's impressive. And three—he knows fashion, he understands it. He likes it." She wound up for the knockout punch. "He wears it."

"Look, I get that you're upset."

"Upset doesn't begin to describe how I feel. Brewster Peacock already has his suspicions about you. If we work together and he takes you down, then he takes me down with you. That man could destroy my future."

"Then we'll make sure he doesn't get a chance. I'll get great shots," he promised rashly.

"How?"

"I'm tall. I can see over the heads of most of those little French guys. Your guy from Milan—is he?"

"Six feet two inches," she snapped.

Damn. "Well, I've got an inch on him."

She let out a breath. "If I'm stuck with you I'm stuck with you, but I am not happy that you went behind my back and reorganized yourself onto my staff. I expect you to put as much energy and thought into your photographs for *Uptown* as you put into the investigation business, understood?"

"Yeah. Of course. I have my professional pride too, you know."

"Good. And if your photos are shit—"

"They won't be."

He heard her breathing out slowly, as though she was stopping herself from saying more. "Okay. Now, for what you'll wear today—"

"Excuse me?" It was his turn to get huffy. "Now you're telling me what to wear?"

"Trust me. I'm doing you a favor." And she gave him

explicit instructions on what to wear. He couldn't decide if he liked the idea of having a professional fashion editor dress him or not. But then he didn't have a clue what was appropriate for most of these gigs, so he decided to let her have her way at least in this. He'd have to watch her though. She was way too bossy.

"I'll pick you up eleven-thirty and we'll head over to the media lunch sponsored by the fashion council together."

Uh-oh. "You should probably give me a schedule of what you need me to do and when. I, uh, can't make the lunch. I'll have to catch up with you later."

"And why can't you make the lunch?" she said slowly and evenly.

"I can't tell you that."

"I am stuck with you against my wishes. The only reason I'm not throwing a hissy fit and getting my own photographer is because I am trying to help you do your job. So cut the crap. Who are you meeting?"

Even though she was mainly acting pissed because she hadn't been consulted about the change of photographer, he could appreciate that she was in a tough spot. Likely there were some things he wouldn't be able to tell her over the next week. But telling her about this meeting was a lot better than having to find another cover story. For better or worse, he and Kimi were going to be working together this week. He might as well start trusting her.

A little.

"I'm meeting my contact at Interpol. We're going to exchange information."

"Interpol?" She sounded impressed. Good. The more he

could impress her with his international connections, the more likely she was to cooperate.

"That's right. But it's top secret, so obviously you can't tell anyone."

"Well, there goes the lead on today's blog."

"Very funny. Where do I meet you?"

He heard pages flicking. "I probably won't need you again until the reception this afternoon in the Marais district. I'll send you the address. You're lucky. Because of space in the magazine, we can't cover every show. Well, I try to get all of them in, but we haven't got space for all the photos I'd like. You'll only be covering the main shows and a couple by rising designers I'm keeping my eye on. I'll figure out what I need and e-mail it to you."

He understood that she was deliberately giving him some leeway. "Thanks. I appreciate it."

"Make sure you break the theft ring."

"I'll do my best."

KIMI SPENT half her morning steaming at Holden. He was blatantly using her and her publication, had assigned himself to her without anyone discussing it with her first and then wasn't available today when she'd expected him to be.

And then he walked into the reception and she forgot her anger.

He looked amazing. Of course, he was wearing the outfit she'd picked out for him. But seeing him wearing pieces of the ensemble in tiny change rooms before the tailoring had been done couldn't have prepared her for how absolutely stunning he'd look striding into the cocktail reception with confidence and even a touch of arrogance.

Damn, she was good, she thought as she watched how the perfect-fitting blazer sat on his broad shoulders, how the fine wool sweater clung to the hard planes of his chest and stomach and how the dress slacks emphasized the power in his mountain-man legs.

His hair, while still untamed, exposed the rugged angles of his face. And he was so wonderfully tall. Okay, she'd had excellent raw material to work with, but the Holden coming toward her, and the one who'd bumbled into Simone's soiree, looked like completely different men.

Then, almost as though he was aware of her stare, he turned and his gaze met hers. And the zing took her back to the first moment she'd bumped into him and noticed the hard body, and then the feel of his lips on hers when he'd given her a brief good-night kiss.

He was the same man, all right, but looking far too much like her ideal fantasy man. Not surprising, since she'd created his look. Still, a dangerous distraction during an important week. She'd have to make sure that business and pleasure didn't get in each other's way this week. Because the way he was looking at her, and the way her body was responding, she had a feeling there was going to be more between them than work.

"Hi," he said, nearing.

"Hi. You clean up pretty good."

He made a face.

"You'll be working with these people, it would be good if you got to know them."

He nodded and she began circling the room with him, introducing him.

"What happened to Nico?" asked Estelle Carmody, a

rival editor, looking interested. She'd been trying to steal Nico—the Milan photographer Holden was replacing—ever since Kimi discovered him, and so far hadn't had any luck. Kimi did her best to hold on to her smile while simultaneously gritting her teeth. That conniving shrew wasn't going to get her hands on Nico. She'd make sure of that. He was her find.

"He's on another assignment for us," she said smoothly. "Which gave us a chance to use Holden MacGreggor." She put a hand on his sleeve and dropped her voice. "He's my latest find. He's amazing."

Estelle had a small, skinny hard-body. No one had ever seen her eat food. Presumably she took her skimpy meals in secret, under cover of darkness. She was holding a glass that either contained straight vodka or tap water. She looked Holden up and down in an assessing way. "And how is he with a camera?" Then she smiled her thin-lipped smile and moved away.

"Friend of yours?" Holden asked when they were once more alone.

She stared moodily after Estelle, who already had her cell phone out. Damn it. Nico had better be on a fabulous assignment, and extremely well compensated, or she could kiss him goodbye. "Backstabbing rival." She shrugged. "It happens."

They moved on. "Ah, here's someone you'll love. Marcy Wolington-Hicks is one of Simone's assistants. She's fabulous." She waved and went toward a red-haired young woman in a black-and-white houndstooth mini and boots. Her only makeup was black eyeliner, her only jewelry a diamond nose ring.

"Kimi, how are you?" she said in a posh London accent.

"Wonderful, and you?"

"Dying for a fag. But I loathe going outside in the back lane to smoke." She grimaced. "Hopeless, really."

"Marcy, this is Holden, my photographer."

"Pleasure to meet you," she said, shaking hands. "Don't think I've seen you before."

"No. I'm Kimi's latest find," he said, sending a wicked expression her way.

She ignored him. "How are things?"

"A complete madhouse. It's all about *The Dress*," she said with a dramatic flourish of her hands. "We've got an entire season of couture, but all anyone cares about is ApplePie's wretched wedding gown. It's pathetic."

"Sure. Completely pathetic." There was a tiny pause. "What can you tell me about it?"

A hearty burst of laughter greeted her. "Nothing. Of course. Simone says she'll rip out the tongue of anyone who says a word." She dropped her voice. "And knowing Simone, I'm not sure I don't believe her."

"I hear there's a matching baby gown?"

"I can't confirm that."

"And you're not denying it."

She grinned. "Right."

"I can't wait to see them. Is the gown as amazing as the hype would indicate?"

Marcy glanced around furtively. "This is so off the record. You know I'd get sacked if this got back to Simone, but you'll find out soon enough. And I know I can trust you. There are diamonds all over it. Actual diamonds. And not any old rubbishy diamonds. Nicola and Mark don't want any bloody conflict diamonds cursing their wedding, so I had to source Canadian diamonds and ask a lot of impertinent questions about the environmental impact of the mines and fair-trade practices. Then I got the okay from ApplePie's people, but get this, the diamonds had to be flawless. Flawless. Do you have any idea how difficult it is to get a large quantity of environmentally and socially responsible flawless diamonds?"

Kimi laughed. "I can't wait to see the dress."

"It's definitely a showstopper. I can't stand Simone—well, no one can—but she is a bloody genius. I think this dress is the most fantastic thing she's ever done. Of course, she's absolutely paranoid somebody will get an advance peek and spill the beans, so it's in a location so secret I don't even know where it is, with loads of security. If it gets seen before the final night of couture week, heads will roll. Simone's making absolutely sure it's locked up tight."

"Do you think—"

"Kimi, and Marcy, my two favorite fashionistas."

The lazy drawl had them both turning to greet Brewster Peacock, whose pale-blue eyes took in all three of them.

"Hi, Brewster. Have you met Kimi's latest find? His name's Holden."

She thought for a second the cruelest wit in fashion wasn't going to recognize the badly dressed, rumpled guy from the Rue de Rivoli, but of course, Brewster didn't get the scoop on everyone and everything by not being observant. Today he was particularly showy in a gold brocade jacket and flannels. He wore large gold earrings to match.

He stepped back and observed Holden, from his neat hair,

to his all-black ensemble, to his Versace loafers. They hadn't done anything to his glasses, but somehow the eyewear only added an intellectual note to the elegant ensemble.

"Kimi, *chérie*." Brewster smacked extravagant air kisses. Always a sign she should be cautious. "I see you've tamed the beast."

Damn. Brewster had recognized Holden. There was nothing she could do but display an amusement she didn't feel. "I warned you, Holden loves to play practical jokes."

"I wonder if someone isn't playing one now," Brewster murmured in her ear, then pulled away and, before she could think of anything to say, turned to Holden.

"Zanetti's a good choice for you. And their prêt-á-porter collection is really quite good."

She was about to rush in and try to save Holden, when he spoke with cool assurance. "I agree. Nobody does a better pinstripe. Classic with a touch of whimsy. Not sure I'm ready for the return of the double-breasted suit, or those wide ties. Remind me too much of my dad's wardrobe. I like the recent trend to tweed, however. I'm adding to my Burberry position."

Kimi could have kissed Holden. He really had read all those magazines. Boot camp had worked! He sounded as if he knew what he was talking about. Whether Brewster Peacock was as impressed with his fashion blather was impossible to say. With an enigmatic smile, the columnist drifted over to a group surrounding Daniel LeSerge, one of the top hat designers in Europe.

Marcy glanced at him in surprise. "I thought Brewster would try and pump me for information like he usually does, and so sneakily that you end up telling him things you never meant to. But he seemed more interested in you two. Are you up to something?"

"No. He's just sniffing around for trouble as usual."

"Well, I'd better run. If Simone sees me talking to you for too long she'll get suspicious." She shook her head. "This is going to be a very long week."

"Before you go," Holden said, "do you have a card?"

"Sure. Of course." Marcy dug one out of the tiny beaded bag hanging at her side.

"Thanks." He took out his wallet and slipped the card into it. Then he offered her one of his. Kimi didn't realize he had new cards. Obviously, he couldn't use the ones he'd started with. She saw, when he offered the new one, that it said simply, Holden MacGreggor Photography. And his cell number. He must have had them printed since she'd last seen him.

"What did Peacock whisper to you?" Holden wanted to know as they walked away.

She was watching Brewster chatting animatedly and never sparing her a glance. "He said he wondered if we were playing a practical joke. He took a stab in the dark trying to provoke me into saying something indiscreet, unless he knows something about why you're really here."

"If he knows anything more than where to pick up Liberace's old wardrobe, I'd be surprised."

"He's deliberately outrageous. It's his thing, but he's also extremely smart, powerful in the world of fashion and very well connected."

"In what way?"

"There isn't anybody in fashion who won't take his

calls. Even if he cuts you to shreds in his column, it doesn't matter. If he calls, you talk."

"Why not tell him to shove his column up his ass?"

"Because the only thing worse than being hacked to pieces in Brewster's column is not appearing in his column at all."

6

"GOOD MORNING."

Heat shot through Holden. All she had to say was two words in that sexy, cool voice of hers and he felt himself stirring with desire. He was naked in bed and the sexiest woman in Paris wasn't naked in bed with him. She was phoning him. He squinted at the bedside clock—and calling him at a stupid hour.

"I don't need a wake-up call. I set the alarm."

"For what time?"

"Nine." He'd been going over files last night, also trying to conduct a little business. His partner, Mandy, was handling everything with her usual efficiency, but there was a theft case they were working that was heating up. They'd been cops in the same precinct and learned they both liked working together a lot more than they liked the routine and bureaucracy of police work. So they'd opened their agency. So far it was working out well. After they'd mutually debriefed each other, and he'd asked Mandy to do some digging into the stolen couture gowns on her end, he'd finally packed it in at 3:00 a.m. Getting up at nine didn't feel like sleeping in.

Kimi gasped. "Nine? But I'm picking you up at nine-twenty. Didn't you listen to a word I said last night?"

He yawned hugely. "Every word. I'll be there."

"I suppose you'll roll out of bed and stuff yourself into the first thing you pull out of your closet." She sounded as though she was hyperventilating, so he couldn't help teasing her a little.

"You could come over and help me dress." He only meant to loosen her up a bit, but the second he said the words he pictured her walking into his room wearing one of her fancy dresses—one of the shorter ones that showed off her legs—and the high heels he scoffed at but secretly loved. That woman had some shoes.

The idea of her walking in here like that had the bed-sheets tenting as he, of course, imagined that instead of going to his closet she'd be overcome with his manly chest—not to mention the manly tent—and she'd climb right in bed with him, high heels and all.

In the second or two the exciting picture flashed across his brain she spluttered a bit and then said, "I think I'll dress you from a remote location."

His grin went wide. "You don't trust yourself to walk into my room while I'm in bed."

A muffled snort. "I don't trust you."

"Smart lady."

"Now that you're awake, pay attention."

"Okay." He yawned again.

"Today you put on the gray Marc Jacobs jacket with the pants by Bottega Veneta. The black-and-white Dolce & Gabbana shirt."

"For a press conference?" He'd studied the schedule she'd sent him yesterday. She'd obviously tried to keep his schedule fairly light so he'd have more flexibility, which he appreciated.

"It's followed by lunch. Rule of thumb. Always dress for the most important occasion of the day if you don't have time to change between events."

He kind of liked her little rules, the way she imparted her lessons like a schoolteacher priming kids on the Civil War. Of course, he'd always been the kid in class who challenged the teacher, on principle. Which had made him popular with the best teachers, the ones who actually appreciated an inquiring mind in a kid who thought for himself, and made him equally unpopular with the plodding types who dragged out the same lesson plan year after year and spent their lunch hours calculating how soon they could retire with a pension.

"Why wouldn't I dress for the most casual event? It's more my style."

"Because you can take off your jacket and slip your tie in your pocket, even throw a sweater overtop to dress down your look. Then you slip back into the jacket and tie and you're ready for the lunch. Make sense?"

"You're a good teacher."

There was a tiny silence. "Are you mocking me?"

"No. I like having things explained. Now I get it."

"Okay then. So, what are you wearing?"

He repeated the ensemble back to her word for word. And the very idea that he could even think the word *ensemble* in relation to his own wardrobe had him thinking he should demand an extra bonus for doing this job.

"Excellent. And for your hair—"

"Oh, no. Don't even go there. I had my hair cut. That's it. End of story. I shower, I comb it. No hot rollers, no straightening irons, no dyes, highlights or lowlights."

"You seem to know a lot about hair products," she said, and he could hear the smile in her voice.

"I've been with a few women."

There was another short pause. "I was only going to suggest some pomade to keep it from blowing around in the wind. Plus a slicked-back look would bring out your eyes and your cheekbones."

He could not believe it. "You want to bring out my damn cheekbones?"

"You have nice bone structure."

There was only one bone he wanted her interested in and currently it was giving up the ghost. His tent was now as flat as a Kansas farm. She wanted him in slicked-back hair and cheekbones. Pomade. Shit.

"No."

"At least blow dry it?"

"Not a chance. I will shower, shave, brush my teeth and apply deodorant. That's it, Manhattan."

"All right. But please take your time dressing. Fashion is an art."

"I'll see you at nine-twenty."

"Oh, and Holden?"

"Yeah?"

"Bring your camera stuff."

"Very funny."

HE WAS READY on time and she arrived promptly. They might not have one damn other thing in common, but at least they were both punctual. She stepped out of the limo before he could get in and came toward him clickety clicking on today's totteringly high heels. These ones were navy with a big bow on the front. And she wore them with a navy-and-white dress that looked crisp and cool.

She narrowed her eyes slightly and looked him up and down as though she might be thinking of buying him for her collection. Then she walked slowly around him. Once back at the front, she eased his collar away from his neck and straightened his tie. "Do I pass?"

"With flying colors. Let's go."

The driver was getting out, but Holden waved him back in and opened the door for Kimi himself, then followed her into the limo. It was luxurious and the privacy screen was up.

"Most of the media will be at the press conference, and a lot of industry people, of course. I've also arranged for you to have access to photograph the models practicing their run-through for Simone's big fashion show after lunch. They're doing it on location in the opera house."

"Good thinking." He was impressed. "If I can get in there with them, I can shoot the dressers and the entrances and exits. I'll make sure I get all the security guards and anybody who seems to be wandering around." He reached over and gave her shoulder a squeeze. "Really. Great work."

"Thanks. Um, you will make sure and shoot the girls too, right?"

"You think the models could be in on the thefts?"

"Just take the pictures, will you?"

He looked at her and suddenly her brilliant stroke of genius didn't seem quite so much like the gesture of someone who was helping him solve a case. "You don't think I can take pictures of models, do you?"

"Of course I—" She stopped. Sighed. Looked at him with those deep, seriously blue eyes of hers. "I have no idea. While you are taking pictures of everything else, do you think you could take some fashion shots simply for the practice?"

"They won't even be wearing the real gowns."

"I know that. But they'll be working on staging, timing, choreography and so on. I've told the house that we're going to do a feature on the details that go into fashion week. A behind-the-scenes kind of thing."

"Terrific idea."

"Except that nobody really cares." She shrugged. "I can probably do a short piece, maybe something longer online, but my job is to showcase the actual fashions. And I need great shots. So do us both a favor and practice on the real live models, okay?"

"Okay." He leaned over, brushing her knee with his hand. "Sorry." He reached his camera bag and unzipped it. Dug around in the bottom and pulled out the instruction booklet that came with the camera. He adjusted his glasses and flipped open the book.

"What are you—"

"Shh, I'm trying to read. Let's see…f-stops. Aperture. Where's point and click?"

She whacked him on the arm with her bag. "You may think this is funny, but it's my career on the line, buddy. You mess this up and I'll be using freelance stock photography. I'll be humiliated. I'll never be able to show my face in Paris again."

"I promise, you won't be humiliated by my photography." He didn't like to boast, but he was damn good with a camera. He could have made that his career, except he liked detective work. Still, the photography was an exciting and lucrative hobby, as well as being useful in his line of work. He laid a hand above her knee, thinking to soothe her or maybe just get her mind on something other than his imagined photographic shortcomings. But the second he touched her he felt the fabric slide against her slim, muscular thigh. She might mock him for his outdoor ways, but she was doing something to stay in shape.

He could feel the heat of her skin through her clothing and he couldn't stop his fingers from venturing a little higher. He heard the hitch of her breath and saw her eyes darken. Making tiny, teasing movements against her thigh until he could feel the muscle quiver beneath his fingers, he leaned slowly forward. "Trust me," he said, and then he kissed her, taking a long, slow taste of her. He'd intended nothing more than a little pleasure for both of them, a taste of what they both knew was ahead, but when their mouths met lust hit him like a freight train. Wham.

Knowing he had to hang on to his control, he pulled reluctantly away, enjoying the shock of her stunned expression and wet lips. "Later," he promised them both.

KIMI WAS INDULGING in a soak in the deep, decadent tub in her hotel. She had a glass of wine in her hand and a knot of tension in her belly. She thought she might as well enjoy this week since it might be her last one in Paris. Sure, her publisher had arranged for Holden to be her photographer so it wouldn't really be her fault if he screwed up, but she'd know her coverage wasn't top notch.

If they hadn't already reassigned her Milan photographer she'd call him and pay him out of her own pocket to make sure she got some decent shots.

She drank some more wine. Edith Piaf was playing in

the background, and whatever very expensive salts she'd poured in the bath smelled heavenly.

There was a knock on her door. *"Merde,"* she said as she was immediately jerked out of her blissful moment.

"Qui est-ce?" she demanded.

"Kimi? It's Holden."

"What do you want?"

"Got some proofs for you."

She was out of that bath so fast, water sloshed to the marble tile. "Wait. Wait. I'm coming." She grabbed a thick, monogrammed towel, dried herself quickly and slipped into a hotel robe. Then she ran to the door while belting the luxurious cover-up.

7

SHE OPENED the door and her visitor's eyes widened. "Sorry. Were you in bed already? It's nine-thirty. I didn't think I needed to call first."

"No. It's fine. I was taking a bath, that's all."

"Oh, that's why your hair is wet down here by your ears." He took one fingertip and traced a wet ringlet. She was sure he only meant the gesture to be teasing, but the second his skin touched hers it didn't feel much like teasing anymore.

He'd changed into jeans; at least they were his new jeans, the ones she'd picked out for him. And he wore them with one of the three sweater-and-shirt combos she'd approved. Excellent.

She saw the brown envelope in his hand and was torn between wanting to know what the contents looked like and not wanting to know.

Curiosity won over cowardice. "Come on in."

"I could leave them." She felt that he was uncomfortable, and she realized he was worried she'd hate his work. Which reminded her that he wasn't a trained fashion photographer, he was an undercover private detective and no matter how bad his proofs, she'd find something nice to say.

Then she'd get right on the phone and wake her publisher up and demand that they bring in somebody else to help with the photos. She had her pride.

"No. Come in. Sit down." She gestured to the sofa. "Would you like something to drink?"

"Maybe in a minute." He walked over and sat on the sofa, but he leaned forward, as if he had somewhere else he had to be.

She couldn't stand keeping either of them in suspense any longer, so she lifted the unsealed flap and spilled a dozen or so eight-by-ten proofs out onto the table. For a second there was absolute stillness and silence in the room. A dozen gorgeous women sprawled on the table, some upside down, some right side up, some sideways.

She picked up the closest proof. It was clear, in focus, perfectly centered in the frame. Already he'd exceeded her expectations. But he'd caught more than simply a model in a dress—not even the real couture number, but whatever they'd stuffed her in to practice the timing. He'd caught the flair of drama in her. Kimi knew the model. She was a young Australian with a guileless wide-eyed stare and cheekbones sharp enough to slice cheese. She had no idea how he'd done it, but he'd caught something magical.

She looked at the next one and appreciated the arrogance in the upturned arms and the way the model's eyes flirted with the camera—or with Holden as he'd taken the shot, it didn't matter. He captured not only her flirtation, but somehow made the dress part of the come on. It worked. She went through all of them before speaking, but she was enchanted.

It was impossible for her to explain to someone how to take a good fashion photo, but she knew them when she saw them. "Holden, these are amazing. I can't believe you could so instinctively know how to shoot a model."

His shoulders relaxed. "Glad you like them. I gotta tell you, I wasn't looking forward to facing you if you decided I suck."

She glanced up at him. "You must know you don't suck."

"I kept telling you that. You didn't seem to believe me."

"You didn't develop this instinct from shooting pictures of animals."

He snorted. "You think there's no drama in the wild? That animals don't have idiosyncrasies?" She kept looking at him steadily. He shrugged, his eyes crinkling around the edges. "And you forgot my work. I use my camera to catch people doing things they'd rather no one saw. You get good at reading faces and develop an instinct for timing."

She went through the photos one more time, feeling the tension in her shoulders relax and excitement begin to build. "You, my friend, have hidden talents."

"You have no idea."

The tone of his voice was warm and promising, like hot-fudge sauce as it hits ice cream, making it melt.

And suddenly she was aware that she was naked beneath her robe, her skin still damp from the bath.

She could ignore his comment, laugh it off, but she had a feeling she'd only postpone the inevitable. She looked up slowly, letting her gaze connect with his. She was beyond delighted with him. It seemed they'd started out on the wrong foot, and now they were learning to work together, maybe trust each other. It wasn't such a big step to indulging in a little extracurricular fling.

"What hidden talents?" she asked softly.

He reached out, it seemed in slow motion, and with one

finger followed the path of a damp ringlet from behind her ear, following its path down her neck. She felt the wetness of her own hair and the dry, slightly rough pad of his fingertip snaking his way lower. How far would he go? she wondered.

How far would she let him?

Their eyes met and held. She'd never seen him without his glasses on and all of a sudden she wondered what he'd look like without them.

"You smell good."

She felt good.

"Your skin is warm."

He had no idea.

He let his hand fall to her shoulder. She didn't move forward and she didn't shrug it off. She couldn't decide what she wanted. To listen to her body jangling with desire meant to throw caution to the winds and sleep with a guy she hardly knew. To ignore the pull of desire meant calling on self-control she wasn't sure she had in sufficient quantities.

He didn't move forward either. She wondered if he was engaging in the same mental process. "Is there anyone at home I should know about?" he asked at last.

"You mean like a husband?"

He shrugged. "Husband, lover, boyfriend."

"No to the first. Not at the moment to the second and we broke up three months ago to the third."

"I'm happy to hear that."

She tilted her head to the side, looking up at him. "You?"

He hesitated long enough that her stomach tightened. As she was starting to pull away so his hand would fall away, he said, "No. Nobody at home."

"You sure?"

"Yeah."

A tiny smile tilted her mouth. "So, we're both single."

"Seems that way."

The moment lengthened, they gazed at each other in quiet contemplation, then he leaned in and kissed her slow and sure, a man who clearly liked to take his time. A man, as she'd seen so clearly from those pictures, who enjoyed women. She let herself go, let herself begin to dissolve into his embrace. His lips weren't demanding, they were more testing, exploring.

The zinging heat that went back and forth between them was insistent. When he deepened the kiss she found herself clinging to him. Her hands around him, her head falling back.

Oh, it had been too long since she'd taken some time for herself, time to let go and enjoy her own body against that of a sexy guy. She'd been working too hard, she thought dimly, but she must have been out of her mind to let this part of her life lie fallow.

They kissed for a long time, tasting, teasing, exploring. He moved his hand to her knee, nudging it open, and her leg bumped the table.

With an expression of impatience, he let go of her completely and turned to shove the table out of the way. A single photo fluttered to the floor, a model wearing something blue, she thought idly.

He dropped down beside her. Cupped the back of her neck and went back to kissing her. He kissed like a man who didn't plan on stopping at kisses.

Waves of heat floated up and down her body as he angled himself over her, kissing her more deeply.

Oh, he tasted good. Strong, tender, somehow American.

When he drew back to look down at her, she reached for his glasses and eased them off. "I love your eyes." Her voice wasn't quite steady.

He undid the sash of her robe and pushed the edges away. He made a tiny sound and then kissed her breasts until they tingled, and the tingling moved all over her. "I've been thinking about this since I first met you."

She chuckled. "Thinking about kissing my breasts?" She tried to keep it light, but already her heart was racing and her breath was coming faster.

"I was thinking about making love to you."

"You were?"

"Yes." He kissed his way from one aroused nipple to the other. "When I saw you that first night with your shoes snapping and your skirt swinging I knew I wanted you even though I thought you only spoke French."

"I—" She sighed, shifting to wrap her arms around him, and bumped her elbow on the sofa. "You know, there's a wonderful bed in the bedroom. Soft, civilized."

He kissed his way between her breasts to her belly. "Maybe later."

"Later," she agreed as he slowly began kissing his way down to where she was hot, needy and open for him.

He took his time reaching his destination, which was both frustration and agonizing pleasure. He toyed at her hipbone, turning that into an erogenous zone, nuzzled his way down her thigh to her knees. Oh, wrong direction, wrong. Other way!

After he'd teased her inner knee, he began the slow, agonizing climb, stopping to taste her skin on the way. She tossed, restless, desperate for release when she felt him shift, felt the warm waft of his breath where she needed him most. She held her breath for a moment, then he put his mouth on her, wet and hot and oh, yes, exactly there. He toyed with her, teased her, taking her up and relentlessly up. She felt carpet beneath her clutching fingers and as she grew closer to the inevitable explosion, her head fell back and she saw the gorgeous long windows, the lacy drapes like a fancy frame and centered in the middle, the Eiffel Tower bright with lights and as glowing and festive as she felt.

Paris. *"Oui,"* she whispered. Then as he moved relentlessly to her hot button, his tongue stroking her to madness, it turned into a cry. *"Oui, oui!"*

She lay there a moment with her eyes closed, absorbing the pleasure all over again. Her skin was supersensitive, pulsing with the aftershocks of passion. He lay beside her, stroking her softly, giving her time to enjoy the moment.

She opened her eyes, lazy and satisfied, and then felt a rather smug grin form. "I'm naked and had an orgasm and you haven't even got your shirt off."

"Guess I work faster than you."

She snorted, gathering her robe together and yanking him to his feet. "Guess it's my turn. And I do my best work in the bedroom."

8

She flicked on a low lamp on the bedside, which bathed the room in romance. Then she dropped her robe and approached him, naked.

She loved how his eyes devoured her and his hands reached for her before they were close enough to touch. She undressed him slowly. She wasn't shallow enough to like him for his wardrobe, but undeniably, the clothes added to his appeal. And under the sophisticated elegance of the clothes, she took pleasure in his body, the hard muscles of an outdoorsman. His torso tanned all over. Long, powerful legs, and a cock that looked made to ride.

"Did you bring condoms?"

His face fell in comical dismay. "No. I was thinking about the proofs. I didn't think you'd be in a robe with nothing under it but steam." He backed away. "Shit. I'm sorry."

"It's okay. I have some." She grinned, slipping into the bathroom. "I was just checking to see how sure of me you were."

"Not at all."

She thought of the way he'd kissed her earlier, the single word *later.* She suspected he'd known, as she had, that this thing with them was inevitable.

She led him to her bed, leaving the light on since, if there was one thing she knew about him it was that he was a visual guy. "Want to know a secret?" she whispered as she pushed him to his back and kissed the spot above his heart, where she could see his pulse beating.

"What?"

She kissed her way down a belly that was taut and muscular and took her time fitting him with the condom. "I'd have had sex with you even if your pictures turned out to be lousy."

He laughed. "You are so easy."

The laugh turned to a groan as she straddled him and took him inside her body. She'd intended to take her time, but she found once she started moving on him she couldn't move slowly. She needed hard and fast and he had no trouble keeping up with her. His eyes devoured her, but, oddly, he used his hands almost the way a blind person would, as though he needed the information from his hands to really see her. She'd never felt such total focus and it seemed to sharpen her vision of him so they were completely and intimately with and in each other. He seemed instinctively to know what she wanted, until she lost count of how many times he made her cry out. When they were both spent, she got out of bed, poured them some wine and brought it back.

They sipped.

"I should probably head back," he said.

"Ah, so you're one of those men."

"One of what men?" He looked aggrieved and suspicious.

"The kind of men who run out the second the physical part of the evening is over."

"I was thinking you needed your sleep."

"I've got a few minutes." She pushed pillows behind her and leaned against them, sipping. "To talk."

"Talk."

"Who was she?"

He let out a huge sigh. "Couldn't you start with my favorite color or something?"

Her lips twitched. "I already know your favorite color. It's blue." Seeing his eyes widen, she explained, "Most of your wardrobe is blue. Also the trim on your camera case." She laid a hand on his chest, still warm and bumping away as his heart slowed down. "So, who was she? The woman who left you fumbling for the answer to your current romantic status?"

He flopped back against the pillows and stared up at the ceiling. A moment passed. "She was Rebecca."

"Rebecca. Pretty name."

There was another pause. She ran her hand over his belly, strong and six-packed from all that mountaineering or whatever it was he did. Obviously he realized that simply telling her Rebecca's name wasn't going to cut it.

"She's a wildlife biologist in Oregon. We met protesting habitat destruction of the spotted owl, and one thing led to another."

She'd left her hand on his stomach and she liked the way it vibrated as he talked. She wondered if he'd ever describe how they'd met. A woman in a flirty skirt and killer heels bumping into him in the Rue de Rivoli wasn't exactly in the same ballpark as meeting over endangered wildlife.

Oh, well. So she was no wilderness woman. She'd fought her battles. She'd been vocal about designer knock-offs damaging the industry and exploiting the world's poorest, and she'd written several articles about the importance of healthy body weight in models. And—

"I'm completely opposed to using real fur, you know," she blurted out.

He gazed down at her blankly, his mind obviously wandering in the Cascade Mountains with the spotty owl and Rebecca the warrior woman.

"In fashion. I also belong to PETA. Just so you know."

A glint of humor warmed his eyes. "Duly noted."

She doubted he'd ever have a reason to tell the story of them meeting. She wondered if this affair would even last the whole of couture week. Tracing her hand up to his chest, she had to admit to herself that she hoped it would. "Go on. About Rebecca."

"I thought she was the one. We have the same interests, got on well, and I figured in a couple of years we'd go to the next level."

"You mean, get married?"

He lifted a hand and scratched his chest. "Yeah, I guess."

"What happened?"

"I hate talking about this stuff."

"Just answer this last question and I promise you can go."

"I wasn't the one for her. That's what happened. She met somebody else." She could hear a raw note in his voice. It still hurt.

"When did it happen?"

"Couple of months back."

"I'm sorry."

"Don't be." He raised her hand to his lips and kissed her knuckles. "Being single has its compensations."

"It does at that."

"Okay, your turn."

She reviewed her dating history as though it were a slide show. "I'm single in Manhattan. Lots of parties, openings, plenty of up-and-coming young lawyers, bankers, some cool artists and writers. Nothing too serious. I guess I haven't met the right guy yet."

"I'm guessing none of those guys are like me."

She chuckled, thinking of the designer suits, wafer-thin platinum watches. She knew men who spent more money and time on their hair than she did. "None of them are anything like you." She turned to her side and kissed him softly. "As the French say, *Vive la différence.*"

"You know what else the French say?"

She shook her head.

"*Voulez-vous coucher avec moi?* It's the only French I know. Do you want to sleep with me?"

She laughed. "*Oui.*"

He kissed her, and then rolled over so she was underneath him. It was almost light when he left the hotel.

THE NEXT DAY Kimi hit four fashion shows, interviewed two up-and-coming designers and went to a luncheon sponsored by a jeweler. Holden was off on mysterious errands that no doubt involved secret handshakes and code words. They met up at a gala reception that evening to honor a retiring designer.

"I like your Kate Spade clutch," he said when he caught sight of her.

Her lips twitched. "Very good. Shoes?"

"Jimmy Choo."

"Impressive. As are you in Valentino."

"Thanks. Couldn't get the second cuff link on, though." He held out his palm and she picked up the simple gold piece and swiftly fixed his cuff.

"So, who is this dude?"

He'd learned all about present and future fashion but had no idea about what had gone before. She patted Holden's cheek. "There's so much I have to teach you."

His eyes smoldered as he leaned closer. "You taught me a thing or two last night. There's a thing you do with your tongue…"

Even though she knew he was being deliberately provocative, she couldn't help the sweep of heat or the satisfaction of knowing he was thinking about last night as often as she was. They might have nothing at all in common, but once they were naked and in bed, their bodies were perfectly matched.

"I had a good time," she said softly. Then realizing they needed to turn their attention back to work, she said, "How did you make out today?"

"Got more details of the last three thefts. I'm convinced there's a connection. Same MO. Always during a big show. A dress gets pulled because of damage or a mix-up or something, then disappears."

"During the show?" That sounded preposterous.

"Sometime between the show and the next time anybody checks on the items. Usually a twenty-four-hour window."

"It sounds crazy."

"I know." He was scanning the crowd, a glittering collection of fashion-industry professionals, celebrities, minor royalty, the rich and the usual hangers-on.

"Do you have a twin?" he asked.

She shook her head. "I'm an only child." She always felt sort of weird saying that, since she did in fact have half brothers and sisters, but the fact that her father refused to acknowledge her to his second family made them forever strangers to her.

"Then your doppelgänger is right over there."

She glanced over the crowded salon and drew a sharp breath when she saw a young woman around her own age glancing around the room like a kid in a toy store. The woman did look like her. Quite a bit like her. Same eyes and hair, which they'd both inherited from their father who right this moment was walking over to her.

"Oh my God," she gasped.

"You okay?" Holden spoke soothingly, running a warm hand up her back.

"I need to get some air," she said, thinking only of escape. She dropped her head, trying to be as inconspicuous as possible. In fact, invisible would be about right. She crept around the edges of the crowd and slipped out the back door to a deserted courtyard. There were a few wrought-iron tables and chairs, but the weather wasn't warm enough yet for sitting outside. In summer, this would be beautiful. Now it was a quiet, dark refuge.

Holden had followed her. She felt his puzzlement, but he didn't ask questions, for which she was fervently grateful. He stood to the side and let her pace the garden once, trying to regain her balance.

Finally she returned to his side to find him looking down at her with concern. She laughed, only mildly hysterically. "You must think I'm completely nuts."

"No. I think you had a shock."

"Pretty smart guy. That girl you noticed? I think she's probably my half sister."

"Which would make the older dude who went over to her...?"

"My father."

"I'm guessing this family reunion was unplanned?"

"Correct again. I've never met my father or his second family. I only recognize him because I've kept up with him on the Internet. He and his, um, wife, are often in the society pages of the Italian press."

"Big shots."

"Minor royalty."

He looked unimpressed. "How could he never want to meet his own child?"

"Oh, don't be too hard on him." Sighing, she rested against a cold, iron table. "He did want to marry my mother when she told him she was pregnant, but she turned him down. She said they didn't love each other and she could manage a baby perfectly well by herself. Truthfully, I doubt he was brokenhearted. He'd offered to do the right thing and was refused. As far as he was concerned, honor was satisfied."

"But what about the kid? What about you?"

"He set me up with a nice trust fund." She shrugged. "What more could I possibly want?"

"A real father?" he guessed, his voice soft.

"Well, you don't always get what you want in life. I knew he had other kids, but I've never seen any of them." She put a hand to her heart. "I certainly never expected to bump into them here at fashion week. What do I do?"

"I could ram my fist down his minor-royal throat. That would get his attention."

She laughed. "But so violent. And Brewster would be sure to write about it and it would be a horrible scandal. Do you have a Plan B?"

"Do you?"

"Honestly, no. If I introduce myself, he might refuse to recognize me. And how awkward for everyone, including that poor girl who doesn't even know I exist. No, the best thing to do is to ignore him. Unless he follows me on the Internet too, he won't have a clue who I am. What do you think?"

"I think that's a terrible idea. Kimi, you have a right to know him, and your half sibs. Maybe they'll throw their arms around you and everybody will cry and you'll all go off to Lake Como for the summer."

"Right now I just want to go back to the hotel and hide," she admitted. "I know it's cowardly, and I won't do it, but that's my instinct."

"Get over it. You've got a job to do, a job you're damn good at, by the way."

She opened her eyes at him.

"I read some of your stuff last night." He grinned at her. "On the Internet."

"You don't know anything about fashion."

"I know good writing when I see it. You're good."

"Thank you." She clutched his hand. "And thanks for being here while I had my little meltdown. I'm okay now."

"Your hand's trembling."

"Is it? I guess it's quite a shock to finally see him in person after…all these years."

"You should go talk to him."

She shook her head. "It's an unspoken agreement. He doesn't want me in his life. I accept that."

"His loss."

"Thank you, Holden. I think so too. Now, you can take me back inside and let's go to work."

HOLDEN KEPT HIS EYE on Kimi when they got back inside the town house, which seemed to have become even more crowded in the time they'd been outside. He watched her eyes dart around the room, locating her father. He knew when she'd spotted him from the look of pure yearning that crossed her face, before she turned and started talking to somebody standing near her.

He felt his fists cramp in his pockets. He wasn't a violent guy, but to even think of a man refusing to know his own daughter made him sick with anger. She was such a great person that he'd been sincere when he stated that not knowing her was Mr. Minor Royalty's loss, but what really angered him was that it was Kimi's loss too.

He'd grown up as one of a dying breed, a happy, well-adjusted kid in a two-parent household where his mom had stayed home to raise three rowdy boys and an even rowdier girl. He couldn't imagine growing up without the sibs or one of his parents. Even most of the kids of divorced parents had seen the noncustodial parent regularly, and if there'd been a remarriage, they were part of the new family.

It wasn't ideal, but it was better than being shut out.

Kimi was busy with her notebook, so he strolled closer to the father-and-daughter pair. There didn't seem to be anyone else with them. He wondered what they were doing here?

So, he'd take on a little investigation side job and find out.

He'd been struck when he first saw her by how much the young woman looked like Kimi. As he grew closer, he thought the resemblance was even stronger than he'd thought. Clearly, both girls took after their father. The hair was part of it, but lots of Italians had that lustrous dark hair. No, he thought what made them more unusual than most people, and therefore so obviously alike, was the striking blue eyes in the sun-tinged complexion.

All three of them had those eyes.

He'd have slipped closer to eavesdrop, but he could tell from here that they were speaking Italian. He was about to go back and join Kimi, when he felt someone's gaze on him. He looked up to find Brewster Peacock eyeing him. The man glanced first to where Kimi was busy pretending her world hadn't turned inside out on her, and then deliberately turned to where the father and sister were. Glancing back at Holden, he raised his brows in a silent question.

Okay, so Kimi was right. Mr. Peacock didn't miss much. However, this wasn't any of pretty boy's business, so Holden simply shrugged as though he had no idea what the gold-jacketed dirt-shifter could mean, and turned to rejoin Kimi. He didn't know what was going on here, but he had a feeling she might need him.

9

KIMI'S TEMPLES pounded with the beginnings of a killer headache but she ignored it and carried on. Maybe her father didn't know who she was or that she was here, but that didn't matter. He wasn't going to chase her away from doing her job. This was her turf, damn it. She didn't go showing up on the polo grounds in Rome. He should keep away from fashion week in Paris. Except, she thought with a depressed sigh, he probably didn't even know she worked in fashion.

To him, she was no more than the unfortunate consequence of a brief affair.

She knew he was at the other side of the room, so she went over to the lavish buffet—very little of the food would be eaten—and bar. An entire table of the most amazing desserts was laid out—an anorexic's hell. And beside them, coffee and tea. All she wanted was a cup of tea.

She asked for tea in French and then turned when a soft voice said in French, "The same for me, please." It was her half sister standing there. What rotten luck. She turned away again but not before the young woman said, "Excuse me, but you look so familiar. Have we met?"

Try looking in the mirror.

"No. I don't think so."

She tried to step away, but the sister who didn't know she existed said, "It's my first time at the couture shows. It's very exciting."

Kimi was twenty-eight and she calculated that this woman was in her mid-twenties. She'd also inherited the fashion gene. She wore a dress Kimi loved that she recognized was by a hot young Italian designer. She was also wearing a substantial engagement ring. No wedding ring.

"It is exciting. I come here every year. I work for a fashion magazine in the States."

"Oh, but your French is excellent for an American."

"Thank you."

Once more she tried to leave, and once more the woman had more to say. "I'm getting married. I'm here to pick out my wedding dress."

"Congratulations."

"Thanks. My mother was supposed to come with me, but one of my sisters broke her leg right before we were to leave. So Mama couldn't come. My father brought me instead."

"Couldn't you have come by yourself?"

The woman trilled with laughter. "Of course I could, but we're a very close family. My mother and father hate to have us out of their sight. You know how it is." She shrugged, obviously used to her life as she knew it, and Kimi gulped down hot tea to drown the shaft of pure, vicious envy that had surged up. "My fiancé is meeting me here in a couple of days and Papa was very definite that he didn't want us here alone. He's very strict." Preaching what he didn't practice himself.

Over the woman's shoulder Kimi caught sight of their father walking briskly forward. He glanced at her and a puzzled expression crossed his face. She held his gaze and saw the moment he made the connection. A look of barely suppressed panic appeared as he looked at Kimi then at the chatty girl beside her. And Kimi had a second to realize that he was trying to protect his "real" daughter from any upset. She'd deal with the pain later. Right now pride took over. If her father didn't want anything to do with her, she was not going to beg.

"Well, I'd better get back to work."

"Oh, wait. You're the first nice person I've spoken to here. I'm Claudia Ferrarro."

The man who'd fathered her was now at his daughter's side. The look he sent Kimi was pure pleading. Please, don't hurt my baby, he was saying silently. It wasn't Claudia's fault. None of it was, so Kimi did something she hated to do. She showed poor manners. "Nice to meet you," she said, shaking hands and never giving her own name.

"I hope I'll see you again?"

She ignored the father. "I'm afraid I have to work. I'm so sorry. Enjoy your time in Paris."

And she moved away.

Blindly, she brushed past someone, two or three people. Holden. She had to find Holden.

Fortunately, he found her. One glance at her face had him taking her hand and leading her to a quiet corner.

"I need to get out of here," she whispered.

"I'll get your coat."

"Thank you. I'll wait outside."

She made it outside and wished she'd followed her mother's advice and gone to law school. She could at this moment be fighting for fair wages for female workers, or better day care, anything to have avoided this misery.

The door opened again behind her and she kept herself turned toward the road, knowing it couldn't be Holden and hoping it wasn't anyone she knew.

"Mademoiselle." The low voice made her entire body stiffen.

She closed her eyes briefly, then turned slowly.

He looked as lost for words as she was. He stared at her, and she thought for a moment he was perhaps sorry he didn't know her at all, except as the woman he didn't want his child talking to. "I'm so sorry to inconvenience you. I did not know you would be here."

"You made that very obvious. And that you don't want me to be here. But this is where I do my job, *monsieur.* If my…presence makes you uncomfortable, I suggest you leave Paris."

He rubbed his temple as though he too was getting a headache. "I thought I was doing the right thing," he said almost to himself. "You had your life in America with your mother. And I had my life here. With my family. I never told my wife, you see." He shook his head. "She is a very devout woman. I did not want her to know I had done something so foolish—" He caught himself.

She shrugged. "Speaking for myself, I'm glad you were foolish. And please don't worry. My mother did an excellent job. I didn't miss having you in my life."

"You and Claudia—you look more alike than any of her sisters." He rubbed his temple again. "It's extraordinary."

"She seemed nice."

"She is. Thank you for not telling her who you are."

She smiled, but without humor. "I've kept your secret for twenty-eight years. I won't reveal it now."

Holden chose that opportune moment to arrive on the scene with her coat over his arm. *"Bon nuit, monsieur."*

Her father bowed slightly. *"Bon nuit."* Then he turned, gave Holden the once over and passed him as he returned to the party.

Holden helped her into her coat then put his arm around her. "Do you want to talk about it?"

She breathed in the crisp Paris air. "I want you to take me back to your place and make me forget all my worldly cares."

"I can definitely do that."

"Good. Do you have champagne?"

"I can have some sent up to the room."

"Excellent."

HE WASN'T SURE what Kimi needed from him, but he wanted to give her all he had. He'd let Kimi take the lead. If she wanted to get plastered on that champagne, she'd earned the indulgence. If she wanted to cry and rant and throw things, he was there to be a handy target. And if she wanted to talk, he had it in him to listen.

She didn't say anything on the ride back to his hotel and she held his hand as though they'd be permanently separated if she let go.

Luckily, most of the hotel staff spoke English, so Holden had no trouble ordering the champagne and, since he was hungry and he had no idea what Kimi might want, he ordered some kind of platter with cheeses and things, and, he said, bring extra bread. He was crazy about the bread.

"Can I give Mr. Armani the rest of the night off?" he asked Kimi, who'd gone to the window and was staring out.

"Yes. Of course."

He pulled out jeans, the new ones in her honor, and one of the shirts that looked like the ones he got at home at Eddie Bauer, only that cost six thousand times as much because some French guy put a squiggle in the pattern, and started changing.

She turned around, took one look at him and screamed.

"What?" he said, grabbing his jeans and holding them in front of himself. "You've seen me naked before."

"Never, never, never throw a designer suit on the chair like that!"

"Is that what you're screaming about? You gave me a heart attack over a suit? I was going to hang it up after."

She shook her head and walked over, picking up each piece and hanging it with meticulous care in the wardrobe. When she was done, it looked exactly as it had when he'd removed it from the garment bag earlier. She even helped him out of the cuff links.

He finished changing and then went to answer the door. After he'd waved away what he thought were offers to open the wine, and tipped the guy profusely, mostly out of guilt that he didn't speak the local language, as though he could buy forgiveness, he went back into the main room.

And damn near dropped everything on the floor.

Kimi was standing there in a couple of wisps of black silk and lace that revealed more than they concealed.

And she'd left her heels on.

He walked forward and kissed her shoulder. "Have I told you that you are the sexiest woman in Paris?"

She chuckled low in her throat. "You know that thing you like that I do with my tongue?"

He grunted in response, since the primitive part of his brain seemed to have taken him over and he was incapable of speech.

"I'm going to do it again. Only this time there will be champagne all over my tongue."

Okay, so she wasn't going to cry or throw things. At least not right away. Everybody had their own method of dealing with emotional trauma, and right now he very much respected Kimi's method.

"Let me get this champagne open."

"Good idea." She picked up an apple slice and popped it into her mouth before wandering to the window to look out at the view. He thought the sight of her silhouetted in his window only enhanced the view.

He poured champagne and walked over to pass her a glass. "Mmm. Thanks." She turned and tapped her glass against his. "To an unexpected knight who rode to the rescue," she said.

"I didn't do anything."

"Yes, you did. You were there when I needed you." She leaned her forehead against his chest. "Thank you."

She sipped her champagne and sipped again. "Mmm. This is my favorite drink in the whole world."

He was a Budweiser man himself, but he didn't figure this was a good time to mention it. Especially as she'd put her glass down, taken his from him and was currently pulling his shirt over his head.

It seemed that overpriced golf shirts didn't rate the same finicky care as a designer suit when she tossed the shirt to the floor and attacked his belt buckle.

She used the bubbly champagne almost like a second

tongue, teasing and tormenting him until he was rethinking his loyalty to Bud.

When he could stand it no longer, he raised her up and turned her to face the long window. He left her in the lacy bra, but slipped her panties down her long legs and she stepped out of them. He tossed the sliver of black lace so it landed on top of his polo shirt.

He nudged her legs apart, stroking his way up.

"Bend over," he instructed softly.

She did, hanging on to the window frame. He could see her silhouetted in the window glass, her face dreamy and insubstantial, the black lace of her bra teasing him.

The greatest thing about his room was the view of the Eiffel Tower, tall and proud and currently lit up. Sort of how he felt. He entered her slowly, enjoying that first long slide, and the way she gasped when he hit her G-spot. When she ground herself back against him he realized she wasn't looking for slow and easy, so he slipped off his own leash and pounded into her.

Their breathing grew harsh, her cries more guttural, below them the streets of Paris were busy with traffic and pedestrians, those little toy Smart cars people loved here.

In a café on the corner, they were closing up for the night, and one last couple lingered over their wine.

He viewed all that while he drove into Kimi's wet, hot, writhing body, while he smelled her excitement and heard her cries begin to build. He reached for her hands and was shocked at the coldness of the windowpane, slid his palms back to her chest, brushing the lace-covered peaks of her breasts taut and straining with their passion, down her belly and finally to the center of her, where he found her so hot. He rubbed her clit in rhythm to their thrusting bodies and almost immediately felt her spasm around him.

Oh, yes, his body seemed to shout as he joined in her explosion.

They slumped to the floor spent. He toyed with her breasts while they got their breath back.

"Thanks. I really needed that."

He kissed the back of her neck, which was still sweat damp and warm beneath his lips. "Anytime."

"I should probably get going."

"Stay." He couldn't believe he'd said it. The word slipped out before he'd thought about the implications. Going from sex to a sleepover was a big deal for him. He didn't ever progress this fast. But, in spite of the idea that he should be horrified, he found he wasn't. He really wanted her to stay.

She turned her head and looked at him. "I don't have a toothbrush or fresh clothes."

"We can send down for one. Room service has everything in this hotel. And I doubt you're the first girl in Paris who ever went home wearing last night's clothes."

She giggled. "True." She hesitated long enough that he figured she had the same reaction he'd had about moving to sleepovers so fast, but, like him, she must know this was a time-limited affair. Outside of fashion week he couldn't imagine them together.

She rolled over and pressed herself against him. "Sold. And tomorrow we have most of the day off. Heaven."

He organized her toothbrush and soon they were wrapped together in bed. She was curled up against him, her head on his shoulder. "You know what makes me sad?"

"What?"

"She seemed so nice. Claudia. That's her name. I have a half sister named Claudia. I met her tonight and she seems very nice. And she will never know about me. What if we might have been friends? What if one day one of us needs a kidney and we'd be a perfect match but instead we'll spend the rest of our lives on dialysis because we can't know about each other?"

He stroked her hair, knowing it was best to let her talk.

"I don't know her birthday or who her friends are, if she really prefers Italian designers or she's just being patriotic. I've never met any of her boyfriends. She's getting married, and I've never even met any of her boyfriends." She sighed. "I always wanted a sister."

He thought of his own family, the noise, the fights, the tricks they used to play on each other, the way his mother would wonder aloud what she'd ever done to be cursed with four hellions. He wouldn't have traded it for anything. He'd have to introduce Kimi to them. If she wanted to experience family, she could do worse. Except of course she wouldn't be likely to be around his family any time soon.

"Do you think they'll leave?"

She rolled to her back and stared at the ceiling, a furrow between her brows. "I don't see how they can. What excuse could he give? She's come to check out wedding clothes. Her fiancé is arriving tomorrow. They can't just up and go." She blew out a breath. "It's a nightmare."

He kissed her. "You've got a week. Maybe he'll get a clue. You'll work it out."

She reached up and nipped his jaw with her teeth. "I think I'll work you out."

So, she didn't feel like talking. When her hands started moving over his chest, teasing their way down his belly, he decided he didn't feel much like talking anyway.

10

KIMI SLIPPED into her hotel the next morning with her gaze focused on the bank of elevators. She'd be in her room in a few minutes and no one would ever know she'd strolled in the front door of her hotel in the middle of the morning wearing last night's clothes. Well, Brewster Peacock probably would. The man had spies everywhere. Her only consolation was that there was bound to be juicier gossip this week than that she'd pulled an all-nighter.

She made it halfway across the lobby before hearing words that made her stomach plunge into freefall. "Mademoiselle Renton."

There was no point in pretending she hadn't heard him. She turned slowly and found her father rising slowly from one of the armchairs and folding this morning's newspaper.

He looked her up and down slowly and a flicker of distaste crossed his narrow, aristocratic face as he took in the cocktail dress, slightly creased from having been thrown to the floor in a fit of passion, the minimal makeup since she'd only had a few essentials in her purse. Her hair was hopeless, so she'd pinned it into a messy knot on top of her head. Her entire appearance screamed morning after and the way he looked at her made her feel like a tramp, which infuriated her. She was the daughter of a prominent feminist. She embraced her sexuality and would not be made to feel like a slut for the same behavior that would get a man praised for being such a stud.

"*Monsieur,*" she said coolly.

"I have been waiting for you. I thought we might have breakfast."

"Thank you, but I've already eaten breakfast." Some devil prompted her to add, "With my lover."

It was almost worth it to see his nostrils flare. She thought he was going to say something stupid and chauvinistic and was almost sorry when he mastered the impulse.

"Perhaps you would join me in a cup of coffee then?"

"All right." But she'd be damned if she'd sit there drinking coffee at eleven in the morning wearing a creased cocktail dress. "I'll need twenty minutes to change."

He inclined his head. "I will wait for you in the restaurant." He indicted the ornate hotel dining room.

She took the elevator up to her room. What did he want with her? Why was he here? She opened the double wardrobe and pondered her options while she dragged off her clothes. Luckily, she'd already showered.

A quick glance at her watch showed she had seventeen minutes until she'd said she'd rejoin the man whose sperm had had a big impact on her life. Even if he'd given her not much more, she had to remember she was grateful for that. But not grateful enough to be chased out of Paris—which she suspected was his purpose in showing up unannounced at her hotel.

Kimi strolled into the restaurant exactly nineteen minutes after she had told her father to expect her in twenty minutes. She was wearing a blowsy Stella McCartney top and black

Prada slacks with her Chanel flats. She had redone her hair into a sleek twist and her makeup was flawless. She liked to spend at least an hour on her appearance, but this wasn't the first time she'd turned herself out in under twenty minutes still managing to look well groomed.

She caught sight of him immediately. He was settled at a small table toward the back of the restaurant where it was relatively empty and there was little chance of any conversation being overheard. She experienced a rush of conflicting emotions as she studied him. Giovanni Ferrarro looked exactly like what he was: an Italian statesman, minor royalty, a well-to-do family man. Of course, being Italian, and a certain age, he also looked like a man with secrets, such as the daughter he did not publicly acknowledge.

He held a French newspaper in front of him, and his other hand held a coffee cup. As he raised the cup to his lips he glanced up toward the doorway and their gazes connected. He lowered the cup slowly and rose, stepping around the table to pull her chair out himself. She walked forward, thanked him and sat and then he returned to his chair.

A waiter hurried over. Her father was the kind of man who would always have waiters hovering and doormen springing to attention.

"What would you like?" he asked her.

"Un café au lait, s'il vous plaît," she said to the waiter.

Her father ordered a selection of croissants, breads, cheese and fruit in flawless French.

When the waiter had left, her father said, "You speak French?"

"Yes." She settled herself more comfortably in her chair. "I also speak Italian."

His only reaction was a slight raising of his eyebrows.

Her coffee arrived and she sipped it, grateful for something to occupy her hands. She noticed they were trembling slightly and her own vulnerability around this man annoyed her. He must be just as ill at ease as she was, but he was better at hiding his emotions.

"Why did you want to see me?" she asked him.

He smiled slightly. "You look Italian but you have the directness of an American."

He was a handsome man, her father. His hair was still full and dark brown, though flecked attractively with silver. He had a good mouth. Firm but sensual and, of course, those eyes she saw in the mirror every morning.

Not being American, he seemed in no hurry to answer her question. He held out his hands in a palm-up gesture. "I thought we might have a meal and talk."

"Talk."

At that moment the food arrived, so several moments passed before he was forced to reply. She took a croissant, a piece of cheese and a slice of apple for form's sake. She and Holden had earlier shared an omelet, which they'd eaten in his bed. Besides, even if she hadn't eaten for days she couldn't imagine pushing food down her throat when her stomach felt so jumpy.

Finally, he said, "Seeing you last night gave me quite a shock."

"It was quite a shock for me too."

He nodded gravely. "I did not realize that you would be quite so much like me." He picked up a croissant, broke it in half and then put the pieces back on his plate. "Or so strongly resemble my daughter."

She refused to make the obvious comment. How could her down-to-earth mother have fallen for this guy? But then he smiled and she realized that he was a very attractive man. Even his voice was appealing. His English was perfect, with just enough accent to be intriguing. Oh, women would notice him all right, but she couldn't imagine her mother—her strong-willed, feminist mother—falling for him, not even when she was young.

Perhaps his thoughts traveled in the same direction, for he said, "I offered to marry your mother. Did you know that?"

She nodded. "My mother's always believed in telling me the truth about things."

"She refused me. Your mother was always so…" He paused as though looking for the correct word in English. "Self-contained. I suppose that was one of the things that attracted me to her in the first place. She was very different from the women I was used to. I was drawn to her boldness and confidence. I was far from home, intoxicated by the ideas and people I discovered at university, and of course, we had no thought of consequences."

He glanced up at her as though realizing that referring to her as a consequence could hardly be flattering. "I did not love your mother, and she did not love me, but I was still very angry that she refused to marry me. Of course, the same confidence and boldness that attracted me to your mother were the attributes that made her so scornful of marrying a man simply because she was about to have his child."

"'A woman without a man is like a fish without bicycle' is one of my mother's favorite sayings."

"I have never understood that aphorism." He shook his head. "However, I had no choice but to respect your mother's wishes. I made such arrangements for you as I felt would ensure your future was comfortable, and your mother and I agreed that we would both carry on as though our affair had never happened." He shrugged as though absolving himself of blame. "I returned to Italy."

"But the affair did happen. I happened."

He nodded.

They sat in silence that was not comfortable. She sipped her coffee, thinking, as she'd thought many times before, that he'd given up too easily. It must have been such a relief to him to be able to run back to Europe with a clear conscience, always able to tell himself, "I offered to marry her and she refused me."

"I wrote to you."

This time his eyes closed briefly before he nodded again.

"You had your damn lawyer answer my letter."

"That was—regrettable."

"Regrettable?" Her voice rose and she had to force herself to lower her tone. "I was fifteen years old. All I wanted was some kind of—acknowledgment, and you had your lawyer write to tell me that contact with you or your family would not be advisable."

"What would you have had me do? My wife knows nothing of my past indiscretions. My daughters, at that time, were young girls approaching womanhood. Your mother made her choice, Kimberley. And I chose to respect her decision. Now I ask you to respect my decision to protect my family from information that could only hurt them. My wife is devout. While she did not expect me to come to the marriage bed as untouched as she…"

"I would have been a deal breaker."

His eyes were harder than hers, she thought. Tougher. "I see that you want some apology. I tell you that I did what I thought was right. But I do regret that you have been hurt by my actions."

"So I'm asking you again, what are you doing here this morning? You asked me to stay away from you and your family and I have. I even lied to your daughter last night since you were having a conniption fit behind her, terrified I might blurt out your terrible secret."

"When I saw you last night, I was too surprised to think clearly."

"You didn't know anything about me, did you?" She thought of how she'd kept up with him, and yet he hadn't had a clue she was a fashion editor who might be in Paris during fashion week. He hadn't cared enough to know.

He smiled, a touch sadly. "Self-protection, if you like. No. I chose to think of you as your mother's daughter. It was…easier for me."

"Until you got a big fat shock last night."

"At first I thought perhaps the likeness was merely a co-incidence. But when I asked someone who you were, and they said Kimberley Renton, then of course I knew."

"Google."

"I beg your pardon?"

"I kept up with you on Google. I've seen pictures of you and your wife at social events, I know that you sit on the board of several large Italian companies. I know how many times you've come to New York on business." Those had always been the tough times, when he was there in her hometown and she knew he wouldn't even try to see her.

"Perhaps I will ask Google about you when I get back to my hotel."

"What Google will tell you is that I'm a fashion editor, and covering couture week is one of the most important events on my calendar." She drilled him with the toughest look she had in stock. "I am not leaving Paris."

"My dear, you misunderstand me. The reason I came here today is to ask you if—there is any possibility that you and I might get to know each other."

She'd wanted that for so long. And now... "What about Claudia?"

He glanced up sharply, then dropped his gaze to the plate. "Claudia has a great deal on her mind at the moment with her approaching wedding. Perhaps this is not the best time to reveal such information."

"Leave the skeleton in the family cupboard, huh?" So, he wanted to get to know her, but still keep her a secret from the rest of his family.

"Claudia's fiancé arrives today. They will be very busy. I thought perhaps you and I might spend some time together."

And she knew in that moment that it wouldn't be enough. She wasn't a confused teenager anymore. She was a grown woman. If her biological father wanted her in his life, he was going to have to share his life with her. All of it. So, she shook her head slowly. "This is a working trip for me. I doubt I'll have much free time."

"All right. Perhaps we could get to know each other a little now."

"Sure. What do you want to know? Let's see. I graduated from Wellesley with a degree in modern languages and a minor in writing. I wanted to go to fashion college, but

Mother talked me out of it. In retrospect, she was probably right. I'm twenty-eight, no husbands or kids, I live in a tiny apartment on the Upper East Side, which I bought with my trust fund. Thank you very much. I love clothes, traveling and Audrey Hepburn movies and I'm allergic to pineapple."

He nodded gravely. "You had that from me. I am also allergic to pineapple." He smiled at her and she could imagine her mother falling for his charm almost thirty years ago. "Fortunately, I detest pineapple."

She felt her lips twitch. "Me too."

"This man I saw you with last night, he is what you Americans would call your boyfriend?"

"No. I met him four days ago." She broke off a piece of croissant, then reached for a scoop of raspberry jam. "Mmm. You have to try these jams. They are amazing."

She could feel disapproval coming off the man across from her in waves and it gave her an oddly euphoric feeling. It probably was delayed adolescent rebellion. She'd never had a father express disapproval over her life-style before.

"Are you certain such behavior is wise?"

"You sound like a father. Are you going to take him aside and ask him what his intentions are?"

There was a pause.

"I didn't think so."

11

BY NOW, HOLDEN was used to seeing the couture set outdo each other every night; still he knew he was in for something special tonight.

There was definite competition to see who could stage the most elaborate events. Tonight, Daniel LeSerge was presenting hats. Hats. And for this the company had ponied up huge cash, and pulled whatever strings needed to be pulled, to stage the fashion show at the Musée d'Orsay.

The best thing about having the event in one of the most famous art galleries in the world, as far as Holden was concerned, was that security would be so tight. They wouldn't want the Van Goghs and Monets getting stolen, so the place would be crawling with security, both uniformed and plainclothes. All the same, he planned to keep his eyes open.

No fancy dresses were going missing on his watch, not if he could help it.

Kimi picked him up in her hired car and went through the usual routine where she checked him out carefully, making sure the creases in the pants she'd told him to wear were sharp, his shoes tied, before nodding her approval. "Can I kiss you now or will I mess up your makeup?"

She twinkled at him. "You would definitely mess up my makeup." And she reached up on her toes and put her mouth against his. He was careful not to yank her against him, shove his hands in her hair or make any of the other moves instinct encouraged him to make. Still, even the brief contact set him on fire and had him anticipating getting her back to his room—or her suite—later.

Once in the limo, he took her hand, figuring he couldn't do much to her manicure and finding he couldn't be close to her and not want to touch her in some way.

"How did you enjoy your day off?" He'd spent the day going over building plans for all the big shows, including the Musée d'Orsay, and studying security, which was extensive and tight, but every net has holes in it. The trick was to find them and patch them before anything slipped through the gap.

She turned her head and looked out the window. Then she turned back. "It was really weird. My father was waiting for me when I got back this morning."

"What did he want?"

"I don't think he knew himself what he wanted." She blew out a breath. "He said he'd like to spend some time with me and get to know me, but also made it clear I wouldn't be introduced to Claudia or any of his family."

He swallowed the crude epithet that wanted to pop out of his mouth and kept his voice neutral. "What did you say?"

In the darkness, her eyes glowed. "I told him I was too busy."

"Good girl." He squeezed her hand lightly, felt her squeeze back. "I can't believe he wants to keep you a secret."

"In a truly twisted way I understood." He heard the rustling of her clothes as she shifted against the leather seat of the limo. "He's got this very stable position, he's a business and social leader with a lot of influence in politics. He's never told his wife or his children about me. I think he wants to protect them from the shock."

"He wants to protect his own ass. What about you? What about what you want?"

She put her head against his shoulder for a minute. "Holden, you're a good man to have on my side."

"Is he going home?"

"No. And I've told him I'm staying in Paris."

"Well, this should be fun."

"Screw it. I am not letting him ruin my favorite workweek of the year. And speaking of work, I can't wait to see what Daniel's created. His shows are always outrageous."

"I thought it was hats tonight."

"Yes. But these are hats like you've never seen before. According to the promo stuff from his PR agency, he says he was inspired by the venue."

"What does that mean? He's going to re-create Impressionist paintings in millinery?"

"Could be. I pity the poor model who gets stuck with Monet's haystacks on her head."

"This I have to see."

"And I'm looking forward to seeing this event through your eyes. Promise me you'll give me all your reactions. Uncensored."

"Honey, you get all of me uncensored."

Her eyes lit with answering excitement and he could feel the heat on her skin as he slipped his hand beneath the heavy fall of her hair to cup the back of her neck. He kissed her softly, dipping in for a quick teasing taste of her mouth before letting her go.

"I am crazy about this place," she said as they pulled up. Before exiting the limo, she whipped out a lip gloss from her bag and refreshed her lips so they were back to perfection and no one would ever know she'd been necking in the back of the car. He reached over and pulled out the travel pack of tissues he could see in the tiny bag, which he recognized to his own bemusement as Hermès, and used one to wipe the corresponding evidence off his mouth.

"Oh," she said in irritation. "My fingernail snagged on my dress. Just a second." And she pulled out a tiny compact that opened out into a full nail kit in miniature. Teensy file, scissors and a buffer. In a minute she had the nail fixed to her satisfaction.

"I've never seen anything like that before."

She grinned at him. "I know. I got it as a gift in Japan. It's the coolest thing ever. I carry it with me everywhere."

When they walked into the crowded art museum, as luck would have it, almost the first people they saw were her father, her half sister and a blond, stocky dude who he would have placed as one of the plainclothes security guys if the man hadn't had his hand linked with that of Claudia, Kimi's sister.

He had a tough-looking face, nose broken at some point, muscles bulging beneath an Armani suit. Boring shirt that Kimi would never allow Holden to wear, and a burgundy tie. His pale eyes scanned the crowd and he had that watchful look that often marks ex-military and law-enforcement people.

At that moment, perhaps feeling Holden's scrutiny, he glanced up, looked him over with indifferent gray eyes, then his gaze moved to Kimi. Holden saw his gaze sharpen. His reaction was barely noticeable. He looked at the

woman by his side and then back at Kimi. For some in-
stinctive reason, Holden moved closer to Kimi and slipped
an arm around her shoulders. He guessed it was his means
of signaling that this twin was his.

The guy said something to Claudia and then she glanced
up. With a friendly smile and a wave, she pulled her
fiancé's hand and approached. Holden felt Kimi stiffen
beside him and automatically glance to her father, but what
was she supposed to do about her sister coming toward her?

"Hello," said the woman who looked so much like Kimi.

"Hi."

"This is my fiancé, Vladimir." Then she paused, and
giggled. "I am so sorry. I've forgotten your name."

"Kimberley Renton."

"Yes, of course, Kimberley."

He almost felt the tension drain out of her body as she
gave in to the inevitable. "My friends call me Kimi." She
shook hands with Vladimir, and then Holden found himself
being introduced and shaking hands all around. In the
surreal moments of his life this was right up there.

Vladimir was obviously thinking the same but he wasn't
going to say anything.

They were just heading toward an awkward pause when
there was a collective gasp from all around and all eyes turned.

Kimi started to laugh.

Then he saw what had inspired the gasps and the
laughter. A model was strolling through the crowd. She
wore an unremarkable jumpsuit in black so her body was
simply a frame, or a base, for the headdress that dominated
her appearance. Her makeup was pale, lips whited out, but
her eyes were done in wild colors, like stage makeup. The

hair was a nest of tangles, and above the hair was the most monstrous headpiece Holden had ever seen. Basically, it was a birdcage. Black, wrought-iron and shaped in a bizarre oval that sat across the model's head like—suddenly, Holden was smiling too. Like a train. Of course, the Musée d'Orsay was a former train station. Daniel had taken his inspiration from the art deco station itself, with its opaque glass ceilings, the black iron and glass. Inside the ridiculous hat—that must weigh a ton—fluttered a canary.

He'd be willing to bet that Tweety Bird had been asleep, a cover over its cage, and as they put the hat on the model, the cover had been lifted, because the little bird was flitting all over the cage, singing its heart out.

Applause began softly and as more and more models emerged, all with cages on their heads, decorated with feathers, flowers, fabric; one even boasted a clock face. Each cage contained a different bird, and soon birdsong built along with the applause.

It was insane. It was magical. Holden hoisted his camera and began doing what he did best. Capturing the elusive images with his camera.

He got the zing in his gut that told him he'd aced a shot when he snapped a sumptuously well-dressed woman feeding a bright blue parakeet a bit of bread through the cage, while the model obligingly tilted her head down to make the feeding easier.

He had that feeling, the sense of weightlessness he occasionally experienced when he knew he'd nailed a photo.

He turned and almost bashed into Brewster Peacock, who looked at him with a calculating expression. "Good shot."

"Thanks."

"I'd love to have something like that to go with my column."

Holden had been propositioned for photos before. It happened. In the same way journalists sometimes scooped their own paper to make a bigger deal, so had photographers been known to sell a money shot to an outfit other than the one they presumably owed loyalty to.

Holden had never had any respect for those guys, or for the people who bought their stuff.

"Thanks. You'll have to talk to Kimi about my photos." He gave a mock salute and went to find Kimi.

She was in a corner, scrawling notes. "Can you believe this?" Her face was shining with excitement. "I want to file a story tonight for the online edition."

"I've got some photos that you should see."

"Let's go."

As they headed out to the limo, he briefly told her that Brewster Peacock had tried to steal his photos. She thought that was almost as funny as a hat designer sending a bunch of models out with birdcages on their heads.

They were almost at the limo, when a voice hailed Kimi. It was Brewster.

"Kimi, darling. Leaving so soon? I want to talk to you."

She waved him away. "Call me tomorrow."

"But it's important."

"I've got a story to file."

"So do I," he called back. Something about the way he said it made Holden turn and glance at him sharply, but the man in burgundy silk was already turning away.

As they piled into the back of the limo, she said, "But his story won't have the greatest photos in the history of fashion."

She leaned forward and kissed him passionately. "Your pictures are going to be fabulous. We'll save the best for the magazine, but we can put a couple of not-so-fab ones with my online piece."

"You haven't even seen the proofs yet."

She kissed him again. "If Brewster wanted to steal your stuff, honey, you nailed it." Not, perhaps, the greatest accolade he'd ever had, but he'd take it.

Perhaps she realized she'd been less than complimentary, for she kissed him again, longer and deeper this time. His head was swimming when she drew away. "Tell you what, after we file our stuff, we can do anything you want."

As incentive, that was irresistible. "Anything?"

She wrinkled her nose, staring at him. "Anything, except that I have veto power."

He threw back his head and laughed. "Has anybody ever told you that you are a control freak?"

"More than one."

This time, he kissed her, letting her know that control was a two way street.

"SOME MIGHT CALL Paris milliner Daniel LeSerge bird-brained," she began, trying to evoke the atmosphere of tonight's show at the same time she described the outlandish creations. Couture week was often more about costume and drama than wearable clothes, and no one embraced the notion of fashion as spectacle better than Daniel, she thought as she typed frantically, one eye on the clock. If she could get her story and Holden's pictures filed by midnight they'd be among the first in the world to get the story out. Even though writing for the magazine was the biggest part of her job, keeping an online presence was growing in importance. Besides, she loved the immediacy of those pieces.

It was silent in her suite but for the clack of her fingers on the keyboard and the rustling of pages as she checked the notes scrawled in her notebook.

By eleven she was finished.

She read her work over, tweaked it a little and then she was done.

Five minutes later, Holden knocked on her door. "Well?" she asked as she opened it.

A big smile and an even bigger kiss greeted her. "I printed off a couple of my favorites for you."

She took a quick look and her body went to liquid. "Do you have any idea how horny I am right now?"

"No, but you could show me...."

She looked at the proofs and her arms came out in goose bumps. Maybe he thought fashion was a stupid waste of time but he hadn't let his prejudice affect his photography. The photos were incredible. In the one he'd marked, indicating it was his choice to be sent on, he'd chosen a photo that made her laugh. A woman feeding one of the birds through the cage. He'd managed to make the image humorous but he'd also captured the sense of whimsy in the birdcage hats. "I'll keep that one for the magazine. I like this one here, with the feathers waving as she walks, and the Picasso in the background."

He presented it to her.

In five minutes, the pictures and text were on their way to New York.

"Okay," she said, stretching. "I'm yours."

"Good," he answered. "Because I have ideas."

"What ideas?"

"Trust me."

There was a pause. A silent tug-of-war took place. "Okay."

He grinned hugely. "Grab a sweater and come on."

"A sweater?"

He shrugged. "Something for the night air." He looked at her more carefully and she thought he was having ideas she couldn't fathom. "Sweater, jacket, blanket. Whatever."

"Why?"

"Because Paris, nighttime and you together give a man like me ideas."

"Why are you bringing your camera?"

He was probably the most exciting man she'd ever been with—no, he was definitely the most exciting, and the most unpredictable. His eyes were full of lust when he looked at her. "I'm a photographer. I might see something I want to take pictures of." His words licked at her skin so she felt like she might ignite, light up like Paris on Bastille Day when it exploded in fireworks.

12

WITH A STRONG SUSPICION she was going to enjoy herself, Kimi walked to her bedroom, threw a black cashmere pashmina into a straw carryall and swapped her heels for a pair of ballet flats.

She felt the bubbling excitement of a woman who after turning in a great article, complete with first-class photos, was now taking a couple of hours off.

Of course, there were parties all over town she could attend if she wanted to stay up all night, but she had a feeling she was going to have much more fun at the private party Holden was arranging.

"Let's go."

"That's my girl."

"Do you want me to call the car?"

He shook his head. "No car."

"Okay."

They took the elevator downstairs. She noticed he had nothing with him but his camera case.

"Any hints where we're going?"

"I've never seen Paris by night. I thought you could show me."

"Paris by night? You want your own private tour?"

"That's right."

"I think we should start by strolling along the banks of the Seine. So American in Paris. There's a moon, so it will be romantic."

"But—"

"No buts. You asked for my help. If you want to see Paris by night, you start on the water." She took him by the hand and they walked along the Seine, where the tourist boats and bateaux mouches were docked.

She imagined all the lovers who'd walked this stretch of river arm in arm. Some destined for a lifetime together, some to end in tears or tragedy.

The night was glorious. The skies were clear, the air crisp but not cold and the Seine glided by like a skater, silent and smooth. They approached a bridge.

"Wait," he said as she started to walk along the pathway that would lead her underneath the stone passageway. She glanced up to see him shrugging his camera bag off his shoulder and opening it.

"I'm not a model."

"Tonight you are. You are my personal muse. My inspiration."

"I've never been anybody's inspiration before," she sighed. "What do you want me to do?"

"Stand by the bridge." He indicated where the solid stone foot of the bridge rested. "There."

She walked over. There wasn't a soul around. The walkway was lit, but dimly, so she still felt the effect of the moon and stars.

She stood leaning against the post and faced him.

He fiddled with the camera then huffed. "No, no, no. I'm not looking for a cheesy tourist shot. Stow the 'here

I am in Paris, having a wonderful time, wish you were here' grin."

"Tell me what you want," she said in frustration.

"I want Paris. I want the mood. This is supposed to be the city of love. Give me love. Give me romance. At least give me sex!"

"You want sex?" She snapped. "Fine, I'll give you sex."

She opened her blouse, not very far, but far enough that she knew the mounds of her breasts would show. She pushed her hips forward and hiked up her skirt. She tried to imagine she had something to sell and he was a stranger, walking along the banks of the Seine looking for it.

"Oh, yeah," he said. "That's it. That's great."

He came closer. She heard the click of the shutter, the snap of photo after photo. She was annoyed enough that she knew her disdainful expression would come through. It kind of worked with the idea she had, and his enthusiastic clicking of the camera was a bit of a turn-on.

"Now, slowly, undo one more button. And look at me when you're doing it. Slowly, remember."

She glanced up at him from under her lashes, felt the heaviness in her breasts and knew her nipples were blossoming under his gaze and the soft breeze. She brought her hands to her chest, and slowly, slowly, slipped another button free.

"Holden?"

"Yeah," he answered, his voice husky.

"Aren't you supposed to take my picture?"

A moment passed and a look of stunned disbelief crossed his face. "I forgot."

"Then I'd better do it again," she said softly, and slipped

another button free. This time he was ready with the camera, coming closer, moving around her.

"Oh, you're good. You're gorgeous," he said as he snapped.

She almost expected him to name a price, but instead he gave her a huge grin. "Okay. Where to next?"

"This is Paris. Let's go up the next set of stairs and see where we end up."

"Fantastic."

She knew exactly where they were, of course, but it was fun to keep him guessing. She started to do up her buttons, but he stopped her. "Put on your sweater."

Without a word, she withdrew her pashmina and wrapped it around her torso. The cashmere was soft against her overheated skin.

Climbing up from the riverbank to street level, they were greeted by the Eiffel Tower, glowing ahead of them. "Wait," he said as she headed closer, across the bridge. "I like the view from here."

"All right."

"Lean forward and contemplate the tower," he instructed her.

She glanced at him over her shoulder, then did as he suggested. "Nice. Don't move." He came up behind her and she felt the shifting of her skirt.

"What are you—"

"Shh."

She felt the fabric shift against the bare skin of her thighs, rising, rising. He didn't touch her, but left her open to the elements, the sky, the soft breeze, the murmur of the river below them. His warm hands ran down her thighs and gently parted them. It was all she could do not to moan.

Anyone could come by at any moment. There was traffic, people looking out of windows.

He stepped away. She could only imagine how she looked, fully dressed, but with her skirt flipped over her hips, her legs parted to show her lacy underpants. Pale-blue lace threaded with ribbons of silk. Her body felt heavy against them, already urgent with desire.

She heard the shutter of the camera and every click made her hotter.

"Turn your head and look at me." She did and thought she'd never known a more exciting man. The breeze teased her where she was so hot, almost like a caress, too fleeting to bring relief, instead it just intensified her arousal.

By the time he was done she could barely hold still.

"You're a natural," he murmured in her ear as they kept walking.

At the Arc de Triomphe, he posed her against the lamppost that said Rue Charles de Gaulle, across from the famous arch, carefully slipping one breast out of her bra and placing her hands above her head.

"What are you doing?" she moaned.

"Shh," he said. "It's art."

There was traffic, even at this hour, and she felt exposed and yet so hot she couldn't imagine resisting.

Once more the camera chattered to her as he took his images. Once more, heat filled her.

"Touch yourself," he ordered softly. "Offer me your breast."

She moaned softly as she complied, staring at him as though she could will him to come to her and give her what she needed. The camera became like a lover, putting

Holden at a distance, behind the lens, so he was like a stranger, watching.

Without direction, she released her other breast, upthrust by the underwire of the bra she still wore. Once more she wrapped up, leaving herself exposed beneath the shawl. She knew he was as aroused as she. It was obvious. But he didn't so much as touch her. Not yet.

Since she was giving the tour, she led him to Place Vendôme, where the shopping was high-end. Rolex, Cartier, and it was also near her hotel. Of course, the gates were down on the Cartier store and here he posed her, under the arched doorway. She thought this might be heaven for her, sex and high-end shopping all in one.

He might have read her mind. "You're waiting for the store to open. You'll wait all night if you have to. I want you to sit on the ground, right there." She started to lower herself.

"But first, give me your panties."

She was going to refuse, this was ridiculous. But she knew he expected her to, so she slipped her hands under her skirt from behind, leaned over and drew them slowly down her legs. She walked forward and tucked them into his shirt pocket, with a little lace showing at the top like a handkerchief.

Then she stepped back, and, making sure it was her skirt under her and not the bare ground, she sat down. He didn't need to tell her what he wanted, she understood.

She eased her legs apart, but not too far. Let him work for his shot. She eased her skirt up a bit, but not too much, she always thought subtle suggestion was more sexy than blatant pornography. And then she leaned back, wrapped tight in her pashmina, and imagined sitting here until the store opened.

She could see the column Napoleon had erected. The bronze plates decorating it were made from canon seized after the battle of Austerlitz, and way at the top, Napoleon himself stood, watching them.

THEY HEADED BACK along Rue de Rivoli. "Nice-looking park," Holden said.

"Jardin des Tuileries, I've never been in here at night," she whispered.

"Come on."

They walked in and she felt the magic of the place. No doubt there were others here, but if so they were being very discreet. Surrounded by the Louvre on one side, the Seine and Place de la Concorde, it was a lovely, ancient park full of trees, statues, a lake and, in the day, crepe and sandwich vendors.

They walked down the tree-lined avenue, hand in hand this time. He found a statue of a female nude, and pressing Kimi up against it, kissed her with all the heat he'd been bottling up.

She moaned, low in her throat, and clutched at him, pulling him against her. She could feel his erection through the thin silk of her skirt, feel the heat of his body against hers. He loosened the shawl, pulled it down her arms and hooked it over her wrists then stepped back. He shot a few pictures, then set up the camera on one of the benches.

"Wish I had a tripod," he muttered, but he was a resourceful man as she'd discovered, and he soon found a tree branch the right height for his purpose, which, she discovered, was to enter the photo himself.

He must have had a remote, for he came forward and kissed her again. Her arms went around him, the black pashmina hanging from her arms enfolding him like bat's wings. She heard the click of the shutter.

And then she lost track of the photos as he began stroking her, loving her. He turned to look behind him once or twice, as though to check the angle and stability of the camera, and then went back to her.

His hand came under her skirt, slipped up her thigh and touched her, just there. He toyed with her, rubbing her with her own wetness until she felt herself shatter, her body hot and shuddering against the cool stone statue.

His urgency was too great to hold off any longer. She could feel it. He unzipped, let his jeans down, hiked up one of her legs and draped it over his crooked arm, and then he was pushing inside her and she thought she'd never welcomed anything more.

The slow seduction by photograph was over, and she felt him driving into her with a passion that verged on desperation. She came again almost immediately, pushing up against him, and then he drove her relentlessly up again until this time, they both went over the top.

13

KIMI WAS DRAGGED OUT of sleep—the deep kind that had been way too short—by the ringing of her cell phone. Annoyed with herself that she'd forgotten to turn the thing off last night—no, this morning sometime—after Holden left her, saying he had an early meeting and she should sleep.

And she would be still enjoying the deep sleep of the sexually satiated and exhausted if her damn cell phone wasn't jangling. She squinted at the call display and then experienced a jolt of panic. Her mother?

Her mother never called her when she was away on business unless it was an emergency.

She answered her phone with, "Mom? Is everything all right?"

"Everything's fine. But something rather odd happened that I wanted to ask you about."

Kimi pulled herself up to sitting and stuffed a pillow behind her, resting back so she could chat to her mother in comfort. "Sure. What is it?"

"Were you sleeping? I thought for sure you'd be up. It's seven-thirty in Paris. I timed the call so I'd catch you before you got too busy."

"I was up really late last night. I had a deadline." In fact, a quick calculation told her she'd had three hours of sleep.

As soon as she got off the phone, she'd turn the thing off and try for another couple of hours.

"A man with the strangest name phoned me yesterday. From Paris."

All vestiges of sleepiness blasted out of Kimi's mind. "What was his name?" she asked, alarm skittering through her nervous system.

"Something Peacock. Oh, wait, I wrote it down. Brewster Peacock."

"What did he want?" She had an awful feeling she already knew.

"First of all he said he was a friend of yours and what a talented writer you are, to which I agreed of course. He said he was writing a profile about you for his column and simply wanted some background. He implied that you had given him my phone number, which surprised me because you hadn't mentioned he'd be calling, but he said you've been crazy busy with the shows and naturally I understood that."

Her throat felt too clogged to speak.

"He said how nice it was to finally meet your father."

She groaned as her worst fears were confirmed. "What did you say, Mom?"

"What do you think I said? I'm not a fool, Kimi."

"Of course you're not." Too restless to remain in bed, she stood up, holding the phone to her ear as she paced to the other room. Every rotten epithet she could think of she lobbed at Brewster.

"I said that I never discuss family business with strangers."

"Good one, Mom."

"Well, it's true. I don't. But Kimi, what's going on? Who is this man and why is he suggesting he's met your father?"

She grabbed a robe off the back of the bathroom door and wrapped it around herself.

"That man is a conniving little weasel who destroys people's careers and lives for fun. Everybody in the fashion world reads his column. Everybody." She perched on the edge of the bathtub then got up and started pacing again.

"And, Mom? He has met my father." She halted at the window and looked out at Paris at dawn. On the street below, a corner grocery was opening up. She watched the proprietors carry out boxes of fruit and tubs of fresh flowers. An old woman walked her dog, a tiny ball of fur who insisted on stopping every couple of feet or so to sniff. The woman wore an old Chanel suit and sensible shoes that Kimi bet she hated with a passion.

"Your father's in Paris?"

"Yep. With my half sister. His oldest. Claudia is her name."

"Oh, honey. I'm so sorry. Did you speak to him? Did he recognize you? And how did this awful Peacock person learn of your connection?"

"Peacock's got spies everywhere. He's got doormen, drivers and maids giving him tips, gossip for payment. Somebody could have seen me and Giovanni Ferrarro together." She turned away from the window and paced once more.

"But you'd think the rumor would have been that you were having an affair, not that Giovanni is your father."

"It's Claudia. The daughter. She looks a lot like me. I guess he saw the three of us and started putting it all together."

There was a pause as Kimi pictured her mother digesting this news.

"You've spoken to your father?"

"Yes. He practically killed himself trying to stop me from revealing my identity to Claudia and then he came over yesterday and we had breakfast in my hotel. He was nice enough, but he made it clear he doesn't want me complicating his life."

"I'm so sorry, baby."

Evelyn Renton had never been the most touchy-feely mom, but she knew her daughter and she had to know this wasn't easy.

"I've got to talk to Brewster. If he puts this stuff in his column—God, what if my father thinks I planted it deliberately."

"First of all, no one who is acquainted with you for five minutes would believe you capable of that kind of behavior and second, unless he's changed a great deal, Giovanni's an intelligent man. Honey, do you want a piece of advice?"

"Yes."

"Talk to your father. He's got clout, connections and a team of lawyers. If anyone can stop this nasty man's troublemaking, it's him."

"That's good advice. Thanks, Mom."

"I'll see you soon."

Kimi ended the call and immediately booted up her computer and logged on to the online version of Brewster's column, "My Secret Closet."

Brewster Peacock brings you a delicious combination of top fashion and dirty laundry. Two fashions that never go out of style and always mix and match.

Then, under the dateline:

Pardon my French, but you would not believe the merde at this couture week in Paris. One hardly knows whether to laugh, gasp or faint at the sheer lack of imagination displayed at this year's couture week, with the exception of the ever-talented Daniel LeSerge who brought a bevy of caged beauties down the runway—and I mean tweeties, not models. Yes, each millinery concoction contained a single bird. One was miffed there was no peacock, but perhaps none of the model's heads were big enough.

However, two darling birds that did catch Brewster's eye were Kimberley Renton and Claudia Ferrarro.

"Oh, no," Kimi whispered.

There was a loud banging at her door, but she ignored it. The banging started up again. She stomped to the door. "I thought you had a meeting?" she said as she opened the door. Holden was standing there looking grim and unshaven. His eyes were heavy from lack of sleep and stormy with anger.

"Have you seen it?" he demanded.

"Peacock? I'm reading it now."

He folded her into his arms. There was nothing sexual in the gesture, it was pure comfort. She sank into his embrace.

Then she pulled away. "It's not so bad for me, but poor Claudia." She gasped. "And Giovanni's wife." She started back toward her computer. "Order some coffee, will you? I need to finish reading this."

She heard him on the phone as she returned to reading the piece. She scrolled down and there was a photo of her and Claudia. They were in the foreground, chatting pleasantly. The photo had been snapped last night. Vladimir was beside Claudia but he'd turned away so his face wasn't visible. Behind them was her father. She hadn't known he was there, but his face registered something close to horror as he saw his daughters chatting to each other. If a picture could tell a thousand words, this one told a million.

The photo gave her pause, and she turned to look at Holden.

"How did you find out about this? I don't think you got home from our adventure and decided to check out Brewster's column out of the blue."

"He called me," Holden said shortly.

"Who?"

"Brewster Peacock. The little bastard called me on my cell—and I would love to know how he got the number— to tell me I'd find his column interesting this morning."

"But why would he—"

Holden looked at her steadily.

And then she nodded, getting it. "He knew you'd tell me. Much more diabolical than telling me himself, of course."

She gripped the sides of the fancy desk where her computer perched. "And he's going to make damn sure Claudia and Giovanni find out."

"So, what do we do now?"

"What do you mean?"

"Do we go to them or do we wait for them to come to us?" He was in full man-of-action mode. There was a situation and he wanted to fix it.

"Let me finish this and get ready. I can't think right now."

The article continued:

Two birds of a feather is exactly what I thought when I saw the oh so lovely Claudia Ferrarro arrive in the City of Lights with her father. Rumor has it that the young lady is a bride-to-be, and where better to buy one's finery than in Paris where ApplePie have spent many a happy hour preparing for their upcoming nuptials.

When your humble scribe saw the fair Claudia standing in conversation with fellow fashion pen-meister Kimberley Renton, he had the strangest feeling that he was seeing double. Claudia's papa, the eminent Giovanni Ferrarro, seemed very anxious to part the two new friends. I smelled a mystery.

While none of the principals in this little family drama are talking, I offer you the following morsels to enjoy with your morning coffee.

The globe-trotting young Giovanni spent four of his carefree bachelor years in the late 1970s at Yale. A young coed named Evelyn Renton was often seen in his company, say my sources.

The lovely Evelyn gave birth to baby Kimberley on February 23, 1979. Meanwhile, Giovanni returned home to Italy where he soon married his sweet Italian bride and produced three angelic girls. It must be lovely for him to catch up with the daughter of his *chère amie* Evelyn, and to be able to introduce his daughter to her. But wait, when I look at the picture, methinks I don't see paternal delight. What a mystery!

And speaking of mysteries, what could ubermodel Natasha Hennington have been thinking? Word has it the former waif has been on a carbohydrate bender from here to the North Sea....

The coffee arrived and after downing a piping-hot cup and a croissant, she showered and got ready for the day. Holden remained, saying he had a few calls to make. She bet he did. His low-key cover, as her photographer while investigating a couture theft ring was now about as low-key as ApplePie's upcoming nuptials.

She came out feeling marginally calmer. The simple rituals of grooming and dressing always helped. Perhaps her life was going down in flames, but damn it, she'd look good on the way down.

She came out of the bathroom dressed for the day, and stalled. Holden was sitting on the couch looking as stern as she'd ever seen him. Across from him sat Claudia, her eyes red from weeping. Giovanni rose to his feet as she entered the room as though even in the direst crisis his manners would never desert him.

"Oh, goody," she said. "A family reunion."

14

"DID YOU KNOW?" Claudia asked in a choking voice, her eyes beseeching Kimi's.

Kimi's heart went out to her.

"Yes. I've always known."

"But I—" She sniffled and took out a tissue. "I don't understand. How could you speak to me and act as though you didn't know—"

"Holden, would you call down for more coffee?"

He gazed at her blankly and only then did she realize they'd been speaking Italian. She walked to the phone and ordered coffee. Then she sat down.

"Let's speak English, so Holden can understand."

"I am very sorry," her father said. He looked as though he'd aged ten years in a day. "I never thought I would cause so many people pain."

"Have you spoken to your wife?"

He closed his eyes briefly and nodded. "She requests that we return immediately, but I will not act like a coward. No. We must find a way to cope with this with what dignity we can muster."

"I'm all for dignity. What do you suggest?"

Silence.

"Are you planning to acknowledge Kimberley?" Holden asked, speaking for the first time.

"Yes."

"Good."

She felt a wave of relief sweep over her. At least the lying would be over. "We could have a press conference," she said slowly. "Take the wind out of Brewster's sails."

Her father looked disdainful.

"I know it's very American and probably vulgar, but we're going to have to deal with the press eventually. You're an important man—an important family. Silence only gives Brewster more leeway to make fools of us all."

Holden rose. "No. I've been thinking about this and as an outsider, I've got a more objective view." He took a step toward Kimi and put an arm around her shoulder. He couldn't have telegraphed more clearly that he was on her side in whatever was going down.

"Here's the way I see it. Officially there is no mystery and no scandal. Both families have always known about each other—" He glanced at Giovanni, and Kimi had a feeling he wanted to say a thing or two but was controlling himself with an effort. "You've just never made a public big deal about it.

"Kimi and her mom have their lives in New York and you and your family have your lives in Italy. But, with Claudia getting married, you all decided to meet here so the women could spend more time together."

"You mean, we already know each other? Kimi and me?"

"Yep. You've known each other all your lives. End of mystery. End of Brewster Peacock's scandal."

"But Mama—"

"I will look after Mama," Giovanni said. "You are right. Of course. I shall go home and explain everything. I will bring her back to Paris."

"But what if she won't forgive you, Papa?"

He smiled sadly. "She would still come for you."

"But Maria has a broken leg."

"Maria will be fine. Right now your mother is needed here."

"Won't she be angry that you're leaving me here alone?"

"You're not alone. You have your fiancé." He glanced at Kimi. "And your sister."

She nodded. "All right." Then Claudia turned to Holden. "Tell me what I can do to help."

"Stop crying and fix your makeup."

To everyone's surprise, she laughed. "It seems you are as bossy as my father. Very well. I will dry my eyes."

She glanced up at Kimi a little shyly. "And then I will get to know my big sister."

Kimi felt something inside her shift. "I never had a sister."

"When are you going to fetch your wife?" Holden asked.

Her father looked rather amused. "When would you suggest?"

"No sooner than tomorrow morning. Today, the sisters should be seen together, and you should all be together tonight at Versailles."

She knew it was a struggle for Giovanni not to rush off immediately to his wife. She couldn't imagine how big a shock this would be to his wife and other daughters after all this time. But, after a moment's reflection, he agreed with Holden.

"Very well. Claudia, I believe you were planning to do some shopping."

"Yes, lingerie."

"Can you make time to go along with her?" he asked Kimi.

She nodded.

"Let me know when you're ready to leave," said Holden.

"You're coming lingerie shopping?"

He grinned, a sudden, lethal weapon that made her knees weak when he turned it on her. "I'm crazy about lingerie. Besides, I'm your official photographer. I'll make sure the photos of all of you as a happy family go out on the wire."

"The wire?" Claudia asked.

"That means it can be picked up by any media outlet who subscribes to the service." She rose on her tiptoes and kissed Holden lightly. "I owe you."

"Let me see you in some of that lingerie and we're even."

THE AFTERNOON WENT better than she expected. Their father insisted on taking all of them to lunch and she chose a restaurant frequented by fashion people. Brewster would find out about the cozy family meal before they'd placed their orders.

After lunch, which included quite a few table visits during which Kimi calmly introduced her father and half sister as though she did it all the time, they left. Her father parted from them to return to his suite where he was going to phone his wife yet again.

The women went shopping, with Holden in tow. It was surprisingly fun. As she'd sensed the first time she saw her, Claudia had excellent taste.

It was difficult to remain formal and shy when you were trying on bras and panties and discussing the merits of various nightgowns for the wedding night. Before long the two were having fun together.

Holden followed them and took plenty of photos. However, he was often banished by Claudia's modesty or his own boredom, and then he took his camera and wandered the area until the women were ready to move on.

They left one of Kimi's favorite shops with a bulging bag for Claudia and a slightly smaller but still well-stocked bag for Kimi. She'd intended to restock her lingerie supply in Paris; she simply hadn't, in her wildest dreams, envisioned doing so in the company of her sister.

As they exited, Holden was putting away his camera.

He looked at Claudia with an odd expression on his face and said, "Is Vladimir meeting you here?"

"No. He had a meeting with some business associates. He said it would take all day."

"What kind of work does he do?"

"He works for an international shipping company. They have offices in Moscow, London, Paris, Tokyo and New York."

"Cool."

Once they'd dropped Claudia back at her hotel and arranged to meet up that evening, Holden took Kimi back to her hotel.

"You're quiet. Are you okay?"

"I saw Vladimir when we were buying lingerie. He wasn't in any business meeting."

"What do you mean?"

"He was with another woman."

"Could she have been a business associate?"

He shrugged. "Something was off about how they met.

They were secretive and he looked nervous. I snapped a few shots but I'm not sure if I got anything before he dragged her off down a side street."

"You think he saw you?"

"Hard to tell. I think he was scared of his own shadow, but maybe he saw me and panicked.

"I don't want to jump to conclusions. Probably there's a perfectly simple explanation."

"Yeah." But her heart remained heavy. She didn't want to begin her official first day as a sister by having doubts about her sister's choice of husband.

It hadn't occurred to her that having more people in her family was going to mean having more people to worry about.

"I wish I wasn't so tired. I could think more clearly if I wasn't so tired."

He kissed her lightly. "Go have a nap. I'm going to take a look at these photos. Find some good ones to put on the wire."

"I was planning to invite you up for a private lingerie fashion show."

He kissed her again, a little deeper this time. "I'll take a rain check on that fashion show. But I'm going to want to see it, all of it, real soon."

And he was gone.

Back in her room she flopped into the bed and dropped into a deep sleep. Two hours later she woke feeling more human. Oddly, the person she was thinking about was Claudia. If Vladimir had a girlfriend here in Paris, what was a good big sister supposed to do?

Holden had three siblings, she remembered as she rolled

lazily out of bed. She'd ask him for the correct protocol. It seemed she had some how-to-be-a-good-sister lessons to learn in a hurry.

She took her time getting ready, choosing a pale-lemon bra-and-panties set from today's shopping spree that made her look closer to naked than actually being naked. She pictured herself standing before Holden in nothing else and was very sure he'd approve.

He arrived fifteen minutes ahead of his scheduled time. He was dressed in the formal suit she'd told him to wear, but she could tell he hadn't put much effort into the details. She'd guess he'd shoved his clothes on while simultaneously running out the door.

"You are hopeless," she said with affection, reaching up to give him a kiss.

He returned it, but with none of his usual enthusiasm. In fact, she'd have to say his mind was miles away. Very flattering when she'd spent so much time while dressing picturing him undressing her.

"Check this out," he said, taking out some photos.

"Oh, these are nice," she said, lifting the first one, which showed her and Claudia laughing over an exquisite peignoir set. She glanced up at him. "Do you really think we look alike?"

"Like sisters. I noticed it right away. It's the eyes, mostly. And the hair. I saw that man-tart checking you both out too. I should have guessed he was out to make trouble."

She sighed. "Brewster's always out to make trouble. But this time," she said, flipping to the next photo, "he's inadvertently done some good."

"Keep going to the rest of the proofs."

She did. The photos were of Claudia and Kimi bonding over silks and satins. She could see how their body language became more relaxed as the day progressed. Amazing what a photograph could reveal.

The last three pictures weren't of her and Claudia. She recognized Vladimir immediately, and Holden was right. She could almost feel the Russian's discomfort. He was talking intently to a woman who was out of focus. They stood close to a doorway and she had the odd notion that he was ready to drag the woman into it should anyone go by. If Holden hadn't had a great eye and a telephoto lens, Vladimir would never have been spotted.

The woman's features were more in focus in the second photo; in the third, both Vladimir and the woman could be seen clearly.

"Do you know her?"

She shook her head slowly. "No. I don't know her." She put all three pictures on the table and moved a lamp so she had extra brightness. "But there's something familiar about her."

"Could she be in the fashion world?"

She wrinkled her nose. "The clothes aren't much. These are cheap mass-market jeans and a windbreaker you could get at Wal-Mart. If she's in fashion, she's not very high on the totem pole. I feel like I've seen her somewhere though." She flipped through the photos again. "If Vladimir is attracted to Claudia, how could he risk his future for this woman? She's completely different from Claudia. She's not very attractive, certainly not as well groomed and she's older. The only thing she and Vladimir have in common is that they both look Eastern European."

Holden came close and stood looking over her shoulder. "I agree. And I don't get a sex vibe from these two."

"No. Do you think she could be involved in his business?"

"Maybe. But I had the same sense that I've seen her somewhere before. And I never get to Paris."

"But where would we both have seen her?" She rubbed her temples. "So much has been happening lately, I can't think straight. I picture her around models, but that's—" She gasped.

"What?"

"I know where I've seen her!"

"Where?"

She crossed the room to her desk, opened the top drawer and yanked out the brown envelope of the proofs he'd taken the first day, when he'd gone behind the scenes to photograph the run through at the Opéra Garnier for Simone's fashion show.

"I used these proofs when I was writing the article, so I looked at them a lot."

She flipped through rapidly. Nodded. "There she is. Doesn't that look like the same woman?"

In the photograph, the woman had a mouthful of pins and she was on her knees rapidly pinning the hem of a model's skirt.

Holden had deliberately photographed as many of the behind-the-scenes workers as he could, which was how he had a shot of the dresser.

He brought over the photo of the woman and Vladimir.

They stared at each other. "So, what is one of Simone's dressers doing with Claudia's fiancé?"

"Doesn't look like an affair."

"No. But it does look furtive."

"Do you think this could have something to do with the theft ring?"

"I don't know. I think I'll do some digging on Vladimir though. Let's see what he and his international trading company are up to."

She'd become so used to thinking of Holden as her photographer that she'd half forgotten his true profession. And that he could find out things about people they'd prefer remain hidden.

15

VERSAILLES, THE PALACE of Louis XIV, the Sun King, was the venue for tonight's extravaganza.

Since the palace was about an hour's drive out of Paris, he'd rented a car so he wouldn't be stuck at anyone's beck and call.

Kimi had gone there early so she could do an interview with the designer. He'd spent the day talking to Paris cops about the recent couture thefts and the intel that something big was planned for this week. He felt out of his element talking to the cops about protecting a few dresses, but to his surprise they took the prospect as seriously as they would if it was a big bank heist. He supposed, in Paris, even the cops were passionate about fashion.

As an information-sharing session it hadn't been entirely successful. They didn't have any insights about who was behind the thefts. The current theory pointed to a Middle Eastern ring. There were women who paid hundreds of thousands of dollars for gowns only their female relatives would ever see. Usually, they bought the gowns legitimately, Holden had seen veiled women at the fashion shows. Was there also a black-market trade?

Mandy was tracking down the possibility of insurance fraud, though that seemed unlikely. There were also a few known criminals the Paris cops had told Holden to keep an eye out for. There was also the thought that couture was to be stolen to be mass-produced cheaply elsewhere, but that hadn't occurred with the clothing taken previously. Those pieces had never been seen again, which left a very discreet black-market trade to those who wore their clothes in private, or collectors.

Claudia's fiancé wasn't on any kind of watch list according to his Interpol connection, but he knew they needed to know more about the guy. Tonight was going to be a high-fashion fishing expedition.

He'd been to Versailles once, on a backpacking trip one college summer. He'd been hungover from the night before. So what he remembered of Versailles was a really bad headache and one desperate moment when he thought he might toss his cookies in the queen's bedchamber. Definitely not one of his better moments as a tourist.

It was nice to see some of the same sights, not with a Eurail pass and limited funds, but with a decent car and in the company of some of the greatest partiers in the world. The Peugeot was slick and fast and the drive a dream. He spent it going over in his head some of the characters he'd met. Simone of the nonstop mouth and restless hands, ApplePie with the relentless media frenzy that followed them like sharks follow the scent of blood. There was that ridiculous Peacock fellow, the big-eyed, big-lipped gaunt-cheeked models, most of whom he couldn't tell apart.

There were the big buyers, the ones who seemed more interested in being seen than in seriously purchasing a couture gown—but with the cost of the gowns in the six figures, he could understand the urge to look and not buy.

He was getting edgy. As every day passed without an attempt to steal a gown, only a few days were left for the attempt. What if there wasn't one? Perhaps their intel was wrong, or the thieves were onto them and not going to follow through on the heist.

There were too many things he didn't know.

Not that this was life and death, but he didn't want to waste a week in overpriced duds he'd never wear again.

As he pulled up to Versailles, he saw that security was tight. Good. He thought it was very unlikely anything would be stolen tonight simply because the palace was crawling with every type of security: electronic surveillance cameras, plainclothes and uniformed cops and guards. Of course, the treasure was the palace itself and its contents, but only a fool would attempt to steal a gown with all this security.

However, he'd be keeping his eyes open, and his camera lens whirring. After he showed his pass, his car was inspected and he was allowed to proceed. He didn't understand a single word the attendant said, but with some extravagant hand gestures, he was able to figure out where he was supposed to park.

He hauled out his camera bag and strode toward Versailles. He paused for a moment when he reached the grounds. They were lit so the gardens sparkled. Usually he hated formal gardens, but he had to admit this was an amazing sight. Music spilled out from somewhere and spectacularly dressed fashionistas strolled the walkways or stood in groups gossiping.

Even at a distance, he could pick out the movie stars. They seemed to have a sizzling force field surrounding them. And always lots of photographers. Fortunately, that wasn't his beat. All he had to shoot was models. No A-list celebrities. Which suited him fine.

He hoisted his camera stuff and proceeded to the palace. As he rounded a pathway, he caught Mark Apple and Nicola Pietra in a passionate embrace. The sound of his feet on the path caused them to stiffen and Mark put up a hand. "Hey, man, can you give us a break here? It's a private moment."

"No problem," he said. "I'm only here to shoot the models."

"Okay. Sorry. You won't believe what the paparazzi will do to get a shot of us."

Maybe going at it in the middle of a public event isn't your smartest idea, then. "You're safe from me. Have a good night."

"Yeah. You too."

As the sounds of mouths moving hungrily on mouths reached him again, he figured some guys didn't learn very fast. Or, maybe it depended on the temptation. If it had been Kimi in that alcove, he'd have tried to get up close and personal no matter how many cameras were hunting them down.

No doubt they were getting all heated up about finally viewing the wedding gown tomorrow night at Simone's much-anticipated show at the opera house.

He was about to go inside, when he was stopped by a British guy he'd run into before with a telephoto so huge and powerful it could snap a private moment from miles away. The guy had no shame. "Hiya," he said. "You seen ApplePie? They disappeared out this way."

"Yeah. I saw them down there by the fountain. And they were alone. If you hurry you might still catch them."

"Thanks, mate. I owe you one." And he took off in the opposite direction to where Mark and Nicola were concealed.

He grinned, watching him race down the path, his camera bouncing along with the fifty extra pounds the guy was carrying on his ass.

Holden was still grinning when he entered the palace.

And then he froze.

She stood there like a goddess and he felt his heart stutter. How could she be so beautiful? He didn't know what she was looking at, but there was a pensiveness to her expression that made him believe she was a woman rich in secrets and mystery. Her glorious hair was up and a dress of pale-lilac silk gathered simply at one shoulder, hugged her torso and then knotted at the opposite hip to fall to the floor. Her only jewelry was a pair of dangling diamond earrings. Her reflection was multiplied in rows of gilt-edged mirrors, so it appeared as though she had a court of lesser goddesses attending her.

The fancy was so strong that he stood rooted to the spot, then broke his own rule for tonight and quietly lifted his camera.

He got off a quick volley of shots before she startled and turned. "Holden? You're supposed to be shooting the models."

"I'm photographing the most beautiful woman here."

She chuckled. "Half the women here have been in *People*'s most beautiful people issue. I think I've got some competition."

He came closer to her, wanting quite desperately to kiss her senseless. Knowing she wouldn't appreciate her makeup and clothing getting mussed, he contented himself with stroking a hand down the undraped shoulder. "You knock me out," he told her. "I was watching you, thinking you look like a goddess. Only you seemed kind of sad."

Her eyes were twinkling, all the pensiveness vanished. "I was thinking of poor Marie Antoinette and how happy she must have been here. Before it all ended."

He took her hand. "This is the Hall of Mirrors. It's one of the few rooms I remember from when I visited in college."

"You came to Versailles?"

He told her about the drinking the night before and how he'd almost defaced the queen's bedchamber with his violent hangover, and she laughed.

As they passed through another doorway, sounds of activity grew closer. While he was shooting models for Kimi's big fashion issue, she'd be interviewing her new sister's fiancé. It wasn't much of a lead—probably no lead at all on what was going on. But as each day passed, each show went off without an attempted theft, the chances rose that *this* would be the day, that *this* would be the show.

"You find out what you can about Vladimir's business, his connection to fashion, anything you can. Try to worm out of him some specifics about his business and travel activities so I can get to work tracing his movements over the past five years."

She nodded.

"I'll follow him when he leaves here. See where he goes, what he does. We'll meet back at your hotel in the morning."

She nodded. "Be careful."

"I will. It kills me not to take you home tonight and unwrap you."

"Some things are better for the wait."

"And some are better when you simply take them." And he kissed her, knowing their passion was being reflected a thousand times.

16

"OKAY, SO WHAT'S going on?" Kimi crossed her arms. Morning hadn't brought them any closer to answering that question. She'd spent a frustrating evening trying to interrogate Vladimir without appearing to. And he wasn't one who liked to talk about himself, she'd discovered when, under the guise of learning more about her sister, she'd asked him some questions. She knew the name of his company and that he'd been to New York a couple of times. He was vague about the rest of the world. "I travel in Europe, Asia, the Middle East, lots of places. Mostly I see airports and the inside of office buildings. It's very boring."

He claimed to know nothing about fashion and certainly his business had nothing to do with clothing.

Holden had been equally frustrated, following the guy back to the town house where Claudia and her father were staying. The father had gone in first, Claudia and Vladimir had exchanged a couple of kisses then she'd followed her father inside.

Vladimir had been driven to a hotel a few blocks away. He went inside and didn't come out again.

"We know that Claudia's fiancé was seen talking to one of Simone's dressers." She paced the room, her arms still wrapped around her as though she was giving herself a comforting hug. "And Simone's show is tonight."

"I'm still waiting to find out what he's been doing in the Middle East."

"You think that's related to fashion?"

"I wish I knew. I wish I knew somebody who knew."

She paused in her pacing. Drilled him with her blue eyes. "I know somebody who knows everybody in fashion—and, damn it, he owes me a favor."

"You don't mean—"

"Brewster Peacock. Holden, he knows everyone. He knows everything. He's got connections in every fashion house, every restaurant, every hotel, every media outlet, every country—he'll save us time we don't have."

"I don't trust a man who makes trouble for his friends. And Peacock made plenty of trouble for you."

"I know. But he also got me a family—" She put up her hands. "I know he didn't intend to, but he actually did me a favor. However, I don't plan to let him know that. I'll play up the 'you did me wrong, you owe me a favor' angle."

"He's scum."

"I don't trust him either, but in the fashion world he is faster, better connected and more efficient than Interpol." She reached for the phone.

He stretched out a hand and placed it over hers. "I'll go with you."

She seemed as though she might argue, then simply nodded and placed the call.

"THIS GUY HAS SEEN too many bad movies," Holden said as they approached the crumbling warehouse in a seedy part of Montmartre. The neighborhood did look like something out of a European film noir. The smell of garbage and strong cigarettes hung in the air. Two young guys who looked to be up to no good sauntered toward them. As they come closer, he saw them leer at Kimi, and instinctively moved closer to her, giving them the hairy eyeball.

At two in the afternoon, there weren't many people around.

That was the only non B-movie part of the meeting, that Brewster had chosen afternoon, but then, they all had to be back for the grand extravaganza tonight, where Nicola Pietra's wedding gown and, if Brewster was to be believed, matching toddler gown, would be unveiled.

They were far from any tourist destinations and the buildings around here were derelict. She withdrew a neatly folded piece of paper from her slacks pocket and checked the address, glancing around and wrinkling her nose. "It should be around here." She glanced across the street where a boarded up store sported a rusty red awning. Beside it was a dingy café with two Arabic men smoking in the deep recesses.

"There it is," she said, pointing. "It doesn't look much outside, but you'd be amazed at where some fashion designers keep their warehouses. They are as concerned about corporate spying as any defense or high-tech company." She stepped off the broken curb, startling a fat pigeon pecking at a crust of bread, and crossed the worn cobbles. He glanced up and down the deserted streets before jogging after her. He didn't like the feel of this neighborhood. The sooner they were out of here, the better.

She reached the doorway and pressed the bell next to a

dented dull-green metal door. Graffiti was sprayed across it and Holden was just as glad he didn't understand the French meaning.

"Oui?" A disembodied voice sounded through a grated intercom.

"Brewster?"

"Kimi, darling. Come up. All the way to the top."

The door buzzed and Holden yanked the heavy metal open for her. Inside, harsh industrial lighting illuminated a stairway that smelled of urine and garlic. An old elevator hovered like a pterodactyl. Without even considering it, they began climbing the stairs.

These were metal and sturdy. He could see that the locks were top-notch on the door, and the windows well secured. He relaxed slightly. He wasn't sure what he'd expected, but the seedy locale Peacock had chosen had all his instincts on alert.

He knew it was his years as a cop and a P.I., but still, he always listened to his gut.

There were doors opening off a landing, but no names, only numbers. Interesting. The stairs stretched up and he and Kimi followed them to the third level. Brewster must have been listening for them, because he opened one of the three doors when they got to the landing.

"Bonjour, mes enfants," he said. He was wearing a purple and yellow paisley coat that hurt Holden's eyes, black jeans and black alligator cowboy boots with gold lacing. All he needed was a cowboy hat and a microphone and he could be a Vegas entertainer.

He and Kimi did the three-cheek-kisses thing popular with the French. Holden wanted to tell Peacock that if he tried to kiss Holden he'd end up with his teeth down his throat, but apparently his glare said it for him. Holden had started out half stunned and half amused by the guy, but now that the peacock had tried to cause trouble for Kimi, Holden had nothing but contempt for him.

He glanced around, but this top-floor warehouse seemed more of a storage area than a secret design studio. A line of industrial sewing machines slouched under a barred window. There were a couple of racks of clothes that didn't look anything like the couture creations Holden was used to seeing, and a large cutting table with a few bolts of fabric. Some banks of drawers rounded out the furniture. A sewing dummy, or whatever those stuffed things that looked like a woman's torso were called, watched from the far side of the room. A closed door led, presumably, to an office or washroom.

Kimi looked around, obviously confused. "Why did you want to meet us here? I thought you were doing a story on a secret design studio or something."

He laughed. "No. But I was here meeting someone else earlier and thought we wanted privacy."

She nodded, satisfied. "You said you had some information that might help prevent a couture theft."

"You know me, darling. I always have the inside scoop on everything." He turned to the full-length wall mirror and adjusted the collar of his pimp coat. Diamonds flashed on his hands and in his ears. Holden swallowed his impatience, but he was getting a feeling that Peacock didn't know jack and they were here on a wild-goose chase they didn't have time for.

He was getting ready to open the door at his back and

haul Kimi out. He needed to make sure the security was drum tight for tonight's event, and knowing Kimi, she'd need extra time to dress.

She obviously shared his impatience. "Look, Brewster, you're not my favorite person right now, so if you have information, you should give it to us. If you don't, quit wasting my time."

"I'm hurt. Didn't I help you reconnect with Daddy Dearest and your precious little sister?"

Holden could have sworn he heard Kimi's teeth grinding from across the room. "No, you really didn't. We've known all about each other forever."

He chuckled. "You're a good spin doctor, my precious, but you and I both know I outed you. Now, come on, let's all be friends and come and look at the delicious gossip I've got for you."

She crossed her hands under her breasts. "What is it?"

"I have definite information that the most spectacular couture piece in a century is going to be stolen." He paused for emphasis, his pale eyes gleaming with excitement. "Tonight."

"Every designer thinks every garment they create is the most spectacular piece of this or any century. You'll have to do better than that."

He smirked at her. "You can't think of one piece this season that is perhaps slightly more special than all the other pretty frocks?"

He watched her face change. Surprise turned to shock. "You don't mean—"

"Now you're using your brains."

"What's he talking about?" Holden asked.

Brewster deferred to Kimi. "The wedding dress. Pietra's wedding gown. It's supposed to be breathtaking. Remember what Marcy said? A bodice covered with flawless diamonds? Even without the cachet of having been designed for the hottest movie-star couple on the planet, the dress itself would be worth a fortune."

"But with its provenance—" Peacock shrugged his ridiculous purple and yellow shoulders "—the sky's the limit. Perhaps it will one day be worn by a bride, but I doubt it." He shook his head. "There are collectors who love that which is so rare as to be unattainable. And this—" he made a grand gesture "—this is the theft not only of the most eagerly awaited couture piece of the season, but it's a perfect scandal. Oh, what fun we'll have."

"There's more security around that dress than around the *Mona Lisa* or the crown jewels," Holden said. "What proof do you have that the wedding gown is the target?"

Again that self-satisfied chuckle. The man had a laugh that was the aural equivalent of too-sweet candy. "Come over here and let me show you."

Holden hesitated, not liking to leave his position by the door, but the peacock beckoned and there was nobody there but the three of them. And he could take that overstuffed parrot any day.

"Here's what I wanted to show you," Brewster Peacock said.

He reached for a portfolio case that Holden hadn't noticed leaning against the side of the sewing table and took out a sheaf of glossy photos. "Ohmygod," squealed Kimi. "Where did you get these? Oh, it's gorgeous." She glanced up. "Look, Holden. The wedding gown and matching toddler gown."

He walked forward, curious to see what kind of wedding dress was worth the fuss this thing was causing. "Hmm," he said, "looks like something Marie Antoinette would have worn."

"Exactly, but she's added an entirely modern sensibility," Kimi gushed. "The way the silk sweeps, and the clever way she's used nothing but diamonds so it has a fairy quality." She touched the photo as though it were the precious dress. "This is the most exquisite thing I've ever seen."

He heard the squeak of a hinge and was immediately alert, swinging his body around to confront—he had no idea what. The door that had been closed opened, and out came Claudia's fiancé.

"Vladimir?" Kimi cried out. "What are you doing here?"

Holden didn't bother asking questions, he was already on the balls of his feet ready to pounce.

"I wouldn't if I were you, Holden," said Brewster Peacock from behind him, and a glance over his shoulder confirmed his worst fears. They'd been set up. Peacock held a 9mm Glock and had it trained on Kimi.

"Shit," he said, cursing his own stupidity for blundering into a trap like a rank beginner.

"I don't understand," Kimi said, sounding more puzzled than scared. "Brewster, what is going on?"

"I did withhold a little information from you, darling Kimi. It turns out, I'm being paid a fabulous amount of money to steal poor Nicola's wedding gown. It's sad to know she'll have to wear something off the rack, but next to fashion, you know I love money best."

"But why would you steal couture?"

"I've been doing it for years for extra pocket money.

But never on this scale. This is my retirement fund. My swan song. My—"

"Your 401K, we get it. Who's paying you?"

Another chuckle. "He has no subtlety, Kimi. Really, you could do much better. I know you like all that uncivilized brawn, but your usual types are so much more...elegant." Then he shrugged. "Do pat him down well, Vlad, before you tie them up."

Only the knowledge that Kimi had a Glock trained on her by a hand that was both steady and clearly practiced caused Holden to stay still while Vladimir patted him down like a pro. He confirmed his earlier guess that the guy was former military. It would be interesting to see what Interpol turned up on the guy based on the latest information and photos he'd sent his contact there. Holden only hoped they'd move fast.

Of course, Vladimir found the ankle knife, the only weapon Holden carried, and he took the small pocket camera from his jacket.

He snatched out Holden's wallet, flipped through it and then calmly pocketed it like a small-time crook. Holden wanted to strike out at him so badly he could taste his restraint. From the cold expression in the Russian's eyes, he'd have welcomed a fight.

But he could hear Kimi behind him, her breathing a little shallow, but not panicked. And because he realized that nothing mattered more than keeping her safe, he forced himself not to fight back.

"If you're going to ruin our evening, at least tell us who's paying you," she said. Good girl.

"Friends of Vlad's. People with deep pockets and good taste."

"What about Claudia?" Kimi asked.

The Russian's eyes didn't so much as flicker. Again Brewster was the one doing the talking. "Poor little thing. But you can be a good big sister and explain that the marriage would never have worked. Vladimir isn't the marrying kind."

Vladimir pulled a chair into the middle of the room. "Sit," he ordered.

"Don't be difficult, Holden," Peacock chided, taking a step closer to Kimi with the gun.

His eyes connected with hers and he realized in that moment that he loved her. Just one of those stupid moments of blinding clarity that come at the most inopportune moments.

Talk about bad timing.

17

HE WAS ALMOST CERTAIN her eyes were telegraphing back the same message. He winked at her and sat.

"Now, we're going to have to restrain you, I'm afraid. Can't have you spoiling the fun, but look at these darling zip ties." He pulled a dozen or so of the plastic ties often used by police departments as temporary handcuffs. "They come in such fun colors. Who says crime has to be dull."

"I think red for you, Kimi," he said, fishing out a couple of the ties. "And blue for Holden. He likes his manly blue, I've noticed."

Naturally, Vlad had to show off what a he-man he was by tugging the plastic grip tighter than necessary as he bound Holden hand and foot to the chair.

"Don't worry, darling," Peacock told Kimi when she made a sound of distress. "I'll send a message to your family in the morning telling them where to find you and Holden. But I'm afraid you'll have to stay here tonight. You'll miss a wonderful party and, of course, the scandal of the century. I can hardly wait. Come now and sit down."

"Wait, I really need to pee. I'll never make it until tomorrow."

He admired her for her initiative in a tough situation,

but it was obvious Peacock wasn't going to let her out of the room.

But, even as Peacock started to shake his head, Vlad made a sound of contempt. "Shut up and sit down."

Peacock pursed his lips in annoyance. He liked to be in control then. Interesting. "We aren't all barbarians," he said, giving the Russian a cutting look. "Of course you can tinkle. Give me your cell phone and your pretty Chanel bag. I'll take you to the bathroom myself."

Vladimir began cursing in Russian until Peacock sighed and turned. "If we're not back in five minutes, kill Holden," he said, and then he led Kimi through the same door Vladimir had hidden behind.

In far fewer than five minutes, the pair returned.

This time, when Peacock told her to sit in the chair Vladimir had set across from the one Holden now occupied, she did.

Vlad did his he-man thing again and when he tightened the tie around Kimi's wrist she cried out in pain. Holden tried to jerk out of his chair, but all he did was yank his own bonds tighter. "Leave her alone, you bastard," he snapped. He didn't remember ever feeling this sense of impotent fury. He'd been a fool, a patsy, an easy mark. And that pair of dress thieves better run far and fast, because if he got out of here alive, he was going to track them down and make them very sorry they'd made Kimi cry out in pain.

"No need to be such a brute," Peacock fussed. "Here, you take the gun. I'll do Kimi." It was clear that Vladimir didn't care for the change in plan, but he didn't say anything, merely took the gun with an expression that suggested he'd like to use it on all of them.

Once Peacock had trussed her up, he said, "I'm very sorry to have to do this, love, but it's in my nature to be extra cautious."

"Oh no," she said when she saw the duct tape.

"Honestly, it hurts me as much as it hurts you," he said, taking sewing scissors out of one of the drawers and cutting off a length of tape than smoothing it over her mouth.

Holden got the same treatment, without the phony "it hurts me more than you" crap.

Within two minutes, the pair had packed up and slipped out of the heavy metal door, locking it firmly behind them.

KIMI LOOKED OVER at Holden. His eyes blazed with fury. She felt sick knowing this was all her fault. Whatever happened to them, it was all her fault. Weakness washed over her and her eyes wanted to fill, but she squelched the urge. She wouldn't give Brewster Peacock the satisfaction of making her cry.

Besides, they weren't beaten yet. She'd done more in that nasty, tiny bathroom than pee. Nobody'd bothered to pat her down and she happened to have her mini-manicure compact set in the pocket of her slacks. In the bathroom, she'd flipped it open and pushed it up her sleeve, above the elbow. Of course, her arms were tied behind her by a plastic tab that looked more like an office product, although it wasn't very tight, thanks to her whiny-baby act. However, the tie wasn't exactly falling off her either.

Holden was already working his chair around and she realized he was going to get them back to back and try to untie her with his fingers, which she guessed must be already losing feeling since he was tied much tighter than she was and had been so for longer. However, it wasn't as if they had a lot of options.

She began doing the same. Or trying to. But with their legs tied, it was almost impossible to move the chair without toppling over. Almost impossible, but she found, with determination and experimentation, she could sort of hop the chair. It was painful, and she felt as though her tailbone was getting bruised. Her arms were already cramping and stiff, her fingers losing feeling, and the duct tape was itching. If she ever got out of this, she was going to track down Brewster Peacock and kill him with her bare hands.

Finally, they maneuvered themselves into positions where they could touch each other's fingers from behind. Good. This was good. But it was only the beginning. He was trying to get hold of the tie tab binding her, but she shoved her wrists against him, trying to indicate that he should try to get the nail file. Oh, what she wouldn't do to be able to talk.

She grunted. He grunted back. It would be funny if it weren't so dangerous. The chances that those two clowns were going to let her family know where she was were, she figured, slim to none.

If they didn't get themselves out of this mess, they'd be here until someone entered this place and, based on the junk accumulated, she didn't think it was anyone's regular workplace.

She wasn't going to think about death. It was claustrophobic enough with her mouth taped shut so she could only breathe through her nose, and hyperventilating was a very bad idea. All she knew was that she wasn't going to die at the hands of a bitchy columnist in blue velvet and a Russian mafia cliché.

Wasn't going to happen.

So, she twisted her wrists until she'd have cried out with pain if her mouth hadn't been taped shut and she was giving herself the worst case of plastic rope burn, and she felt the nail file shift. Yes.

She could do this. A little more. She squeezed her eyes shut and tried to make the gap just a little wider. Surely plastic could stretch if you tried hard enough. Not thinking of the pain, only of freedom, she kept pulling and suddenly, the file emerged so she felt its sharp point against her fingertips.

And so did Holden. Immediately, he began working the compact down and then he took the file between his cold fingers and together they worked it out until it was in his hands. She felt him move the compact until he came to the tiny scissors.

How he did it she'd never know. But somehow he managed to get the little scissors and start working on the plastic.

Please let this work.

She could hear tiny clicks behind her and felt the heat coming off Holden's body as he concentrated, but had no idea if anything was happening. She couldn't see behind her and Holden couldn't see. But sometimes, you simply had to have faith.

There was something capable about Holden. He was the kind of guy who could make fire from two sticks without breaking a sweat, he could survive in the woods. He'd been so cool during the recent altercation with the two stooges that she had to wonder about his background.

Somehow, she thought, if anyone could cut through plastic bonds with a mini-manicure set it would be him.

But it wasn't a fast process. After a long while when she'd

started cataloging every Chanel suit and the subtle changes each year, and then done a photographic catalog in her mind of every pair of shoes she'd ever owned and loved, not owned and coveted, or owned and regretted—fortunately few in number—she moved on to teasing her mind with fashion trivia. Anything to keep her mind off the agonizing numbness in her hands and the stiffness in her muscles.

By now, the light was fading. It was early evening, she supposed, and, naturally, Peacock and Vladimir, or should that be Vladimir and Peacock, which made them sound like magicians, circus performers or ventriloquist and dummy, had not left a light burning. If they didn't get free soon, it would be dark, and getting through that locked door in pitch darkness was going to be even tougher than escaping in the light.

Okay, don't think of the door, she scolded herself as a bubble of panic formed and tried to rise. Was the tie feeling looser? She thought perhaps it was. She strained against the bonds and, while they didn't snap open, she definitely felt some movement.

Patience had never been her dominant virtue.

Okay. Tired of fashion, she thought back to the moment when she'd first bumped into Holden and then tried to catalog every moment they'd spent together. It was surprisingly easy to do, mainly because they'd known each other less than a week. Yet she already knew so much about him. That he loved the outdoors passionately, was a talented and inventive lover, an inspired photographer and a man with integrity.

She knew he liked his coffee black, preferred beer to wine, plain food to fancy and that there was a ticklish spot above his hip that drove him crazy if she wanted to torment him. He could talk seriously and brilliantly about environmental destruction and she knew he put time and money into his causes, but he wasn't a doom-and-gloom type. He was mostly optimistic about the future of the planet and believed that people would save the earth before it was too late. Then, as suddenly as he'd gone all serious on her, he'd laugh at a corny joke, or tease her into bed again.

He was a complex man, and one who she thought she could spend a lot of weeks getting to know.

If only they had a future. But, even supposing they could get out of here alive, there couldn't be two people with less in common.

Still, she thought she'd be perfectly happy just knowing he was out there alive and living his life. And for him to do that, they had to get free.

She could feel his fingers getting sweaty with the effort, and once, terrifyingly, she felt the compact slide, scooping her fingers at the last second to catch the thing.

She closed her eyes and breathed slowly. She felt him trying to flex his fingers then, carefully, he took the compact back.

A few minutes later, she felt the plastic loosen a little more. She yanked her hands, heard a final snip of scissor on plastic, then felt the final piece of plastic holding her tear.

Her hands were free.

18

IT WAS SUCH A SHOCK that it took her a moment to realize she was halfway to freedom. She rubbed her hands to get some feeling back and then yanked off the tape from her mouth, trying not to cry out with the pain.

Oh, what a relief to have her mouth back.

Taking the compact from Holden, she turned to her feet. Her hands were clumsy from being tied up, but with a lot of cursing and two broken nails, she managed to cut through the plastic and get her feet free. She bolted from her chair and ripped the tape off Holden's mouth. "You okay?"

"Yeah." He moved his mouth. "But I won't have to shave for the next six months. You?"

"Fine. I love you."

He grinned at her. "Not the time or place I'd have chosen, but right back at you."

She kissed him quickly, just because she could, and then went to the rack of drawers where she'd seen Peacock with the scissors. Sure enough, they were still there. A good sharp pair of sewing scissors. It took her all of two minutes to get Holden free. He took a minute to rub circulation back into his hands and feet and then went swiftly to the door.

Of course, it was locked from the outside with no mechanism to unlock the door from the inside. The notion of illegal sweatshops flipped into her mind only to be banished. No time to think of that now.

"Can you get me that nail file?"

"Sure."

She got it off the floor where it had fallen and passed it to him.

"Thanks. If you've got a hairpin or some kind of hook, that would be great."

She went back into the supply drawers and returned with a selection of heavy darning-type needles, a small crochet hook and a stitch ripper.

The light in the room was dimming fast, but he didn't seem worried. He worked the nail file and a darning needle and, after swearing liberally and wiping his hands on his pants twice, he suddenly beamed at her.

He rose and putting his finger to his lips, opened the door carefully. But there wasn't a soul outside. She saw him glance around in surprise and she had a feeling he was insulted that Brewster hadn't considered the need for a guard on the door.

She wasn't macho enough to care. She wanted out of this awful place and she wanted it now.

Holden went down the stairs ahead of her. He moved swiftly, quietly, holding the sewing scissors in his hand, since they were the closest thing to a weapon that he had been able to find.

Her heart pounded painfully against her ribs, and she felt exposed and vulnerable as they crept past each landing with its trio of blank doors. But none of the doors opened, no armed goons rushed out to stop them. In fact, as they crept down the metal stairs she got the sense that they were alone in the building.

Still, Holden was cautious. He opened the metal door of the lowest floor, and peeked carefully outside, surveying the street for a few minutes. Staying still and quiet behind him was one of the toughest things she'd ever done, her urge to run was that strong.

At last he signaled her forward. It was much darker than when they'd arrived and she liked the neighborhood even less. It seemed sinister to her now, forbidding, as though every derelict building housed a hundred unfriendly eyes peering down at her.

"You okay?" he asked softly, his arm around her shoulders.

She wasn't going to fall apart now, she told herself. They still had work to do. Later, she'd find a nice bar somewhere and order herself a very large brandy. But for now, she said, "Yeah," and pretended she didn't notice the burning in her wrists or the jumpy feeling in her stomach. They walked a couple of blocks. A tiny police van roared past them with its lights flashing and its toy-sounding horn blaring, but Holden made no attempt to get the driver's attention, if that were even possible. No taxis went by, nothing but regular traffic. "We could take the metro," she said, noticing a station, then realizing they didn't even have a single Euro between them. Vladimir and Peacock had taken all their money as well as their cell phones. She could try to explain the situation and sweet-talk a metro ticket seller into letting her and Holden ride free, but right now she didn't think she had the energy. Besides, he didn't seem enamored of the idea.

They kept walking until they reached a touristy area. The Sacré-Coeur rose above them and she felt marginally safer. Taxis were as abundant here as ants at a picnic and Holden quickly found them one and helped her inside.

Once at her hotel, he waited with the unimpressed cab-driver while she ran in, got a replacement key to her room and retrieved the wad of cash she'd put in her room safe.

She paid the driver, and Holden got out of the cab, barely getting his feet on the pavement before it roared away. His tux was hanging in her closet, for which she was profoundly grateful.

Once they were inside her room, she said, "You need to call the cops. Simone's show will start any second."

"Dress for the show. Fast."

"But—"

"No cops. Trust me, Kimi. I know what I'm doing. I watched the run-through. Don't worry. We'll make it."

She broke every one of her own speed records and was dressed and ready to go in under ten minutes. Refusing to let her call the car, so Brewster and Vladimir would have no reason for suspicion, he got them a taxi at the front of the hotel.

"We should call the police," she said again, once they were roaring toward the opera house, but he shook his head. "Holden—" she put her hand on his arm "—we're probably too late."

He touched her face. "We're not too late. We'll get them. But I'd rather catch them red-handed in front of a lot of witnesses. Don't worry."

She tried not to, but it was tough. As the cab drew closer, she almost expected to see Nicola Pietra racing down the street, distraught, searching for her wedding gown, and hysterical fashionistas running around like a Greek chorus of fashion doom.

But the streets were free of drama, though the traffic grew busier as they approached the opera house.

"How are we going to do this? What if Brewster or Vladimir sees us?"

"Then they'll call off the theft. We can't let them see us. Not until we're ready."

"You already have a plan."

"I'm trying to think of one. But you keep talking and distracting me."

"Oh. Sorry. I talk when I'm nervous."

"I noticed."

"I'll stop talking then and let you think."

"Thank you."

She let a couple of minutes pass. The taxi roared past street after street of elegant apartments. Soon they'd be there. A part of her would be quite happy if Brewster and Vlad the Fashion Week Destroyer saw them and called off the theft. Because trying to catch them in the act was going to be a delicate matter of timing and stealth. And the fact that the two had been happy to leave them tied up most likely to die, suggested they'd be ruthless if they were thwarted. Tonight could easily turn dangerous. And her family was involved. Someone could get hurt. She turned her head and looked at Holden beside her, obviously deep in planning mode.

Most likely the person who would be hurt would be him, and she couldn't bear the thought of that. She remembered the guns.

He asked the cabdriver to stop by a junky tourist store that was still open. He ran inside before she could scold him for delaying them further.

"We should call the police," she said again when he returned with a brown paper bag. "They can take care of this."

He shook his head. "Our buddies get a sniff of the gendarmes and they'll pull the plug."

"But we know what they tried to do."

He shook his head. "Our word against theirs. Not enough to stop them. Not enough to convict."

"So you have to put yourself in danger?" Her voice rose, but she was beyond caring.

He sent her a half smile. "I'm good at what I do." Then he was all business. "How well do you know the opera house?"

"I've seen *Phantom of the Opera*. I know the interior is spectacular, and the place is supposed to be haunted."

"Below there's a warren of change rooms and storerooms. Lots of hiding places, but they'll prefer getting the dress off-site." He looked at her. "If you were going to steal that dress, and you had a dresser onside, how would you do it?"

"It's mayhem backstage, people everywhere—models, dressers, emergency seamstresses, the director, the designers, the hair and makeup people, the staging crew, there's security."

He nodded.

"They must be using the dresser to get the wedding gown out of there."

"I agree. But how?"

She drummed her fingernails against her bag. "The dressers get treated like crap by the high-maintenance models and it's like they're invisible to most everyone else. The dresser will be in charge of the gown. She'll have a list of all the accessories, shoes, jewelry that go with it. It will be her responsibility to make sure the dress is perfect when the model steps out onto the runway."

Wow. It was so simple.

"A hem gets loose, some trim gets damaged, sometimes in the rush a model puts her heel through the fabric. Then the dresser has to run the gown back to a seamstress. It usually means the order of the show gets changed, or if it's too badly damaged, they would remove the gown from the program."

"They won't remove ApplePie's wedding gown from the program."

"No."

She leaned forward, as if she could urge the cab on by redistributing her body weight farther forward.

"How many wedding gowns were in the final segment of the show? When you watched the run-through? Do you remember?"

He closed his eyes. "Eight."

"And they'll bring that gown out last. There will be tons of attention on it, so the model will be out there longer. Then she'll go back and they'll do the finale. With all the models. And that gown as the centerpiece of the show, with Simone proudly hovering over it."

"So when's the dresser's opportunity?"

"After the wedding gowns start showing. She'll make sure there's a tear or something and run it back to the seamstress. She'll put it inside a bag so it's not obvious what she's got. And instead of going for the seamstress, she flees with the dress to an outside exit. Where there's a van waiting.

There are vans and delivery vehicles all over the place. She jumps in the van with the dress. It's minutes before anyone notices the theft. Holden, she could be miles away before anyone notices. At least alert the security guys."

"Can't. If you're right, how does she get past security to get outside to the waiting van? They need more than one dresser on the payroll to execute this. They've got somebody in the security team too."

She was about to speak, when the cab came to a jerking halt that had Kimi bracing her arms against the back of the front seat to stop from being thrown onto the floor.

19

"ATTENTION!" she cried to the crazy driver.

The driver gesticulated and swore, pointing out the front window of the cab.

"Merde," she said, immediately seeing the trouble. On the road ahead two vans had collided. With no room to drive around the mess, the driver stuck his head out the window and added his voice to the mix of shouting.

"This is going to take a while. We'll have to go the rest of the way on foot," she told Holden.

He was out of his side, throwing money at the driver, while she got out the other side. The opera house gleamed like the rich jewel it was, but it was several blocks away and her heels were not made for sprinting.

"Come on," he said, already jogging.

"The things I do for fashion." She bent over and took off one very expensive Jimmy Choo and then the other. Holding them in her hand by the silver straps, she took Holden's hand and began to run. The pavement was rough beneath her feet and cold, and she tried very hard not to think of all the gross and disgusting substances she was probably running on.

"Go on ahead," she shouted when she could see that he was holding himself back for her.

"No. We've got time. We'll make it."

So they ran. Obviously he was in better shape than she was since she was using up all her energy to keep breathing and moving at the same time, and he could do both with ease while outlining a plan of action like a general before a big battle.

The opera house grew closer, gleaming gold in the lights.

"You've got it?" he asked her.

"Yes," she panted.

"Good. Keep your eyes open, but don't get close enough for them to see you."

"Right. But the two of us can't stop them all by ourselves."

He squeezed her hand. "I called my buddy at Interpol. He's sending some guys who won't be recognized." He checked his watch. "They should be here any minute."

She nodded.

He took out a kid's whistle from the brown paper bag he was holding. It was like the gendarme whistles as seen in *The Pink Panther* movies. He solemnly hooked hers over her neck. "A cell phone would be better, but blow your whistle if you need me."

"Okay."

He kissed her once, hard and fast. Then they split up as arranged and she walked the perimeter of the opera house going clockwise, while he went counterclockwise. She slipped her shoes back on since she'd look less peculiar than if she was caught skulking by back entrances with a pair of heels in her hand. She tried to keep to the shadows.

There were vans everywhere, of course, parked haphazardly, with barely enough room for anyone to drive out of the area.

She kept her eyes open for Vladimir or Brewster, but saw neither. In fact, she saw no one more sinister than a few burly drivers slouching in their vehicles who gave her the once-over. But nobody approached or spoke to her, no dresser came flying out a door with a priceless wedding gown bunched in her hands.

The word she'd have to use to sum up her current feelings would be *anticlimax.*

It took her fifteen minutes of eyes-focused, ears-straining sleuthing to discover that everything was peaceful. She rounded a corner and saw Holden coming her way, shaking his head. Even his camera bag drooped with disappointment.

"We've worked too hard to let them win. I'm going inside," she said. "Through the back."

He nodded briefly. "I'm coming with you."

She raised her brows, but he jerked his head in the direction of his camera bag. "I shot the run-through, remember? They all know me."

"Okay."

She showed her credentials at the door to a bored security guard who shook his head. Nobody allowed in.

There was no point in telling some story about writing an article from backstage. The security guard wouldn't believe it, and if he did he wouldn't care. She saw Holden start reaching for his wallet.

"Can you reach Marcy Wolington-Hicks?" she asked the guy. "It's important. Tell her Kimi Renton needs to see her right away."

The man looked as though he was still going to refuse, when Holden slipped him a bill. It was in the guy's pocket so fast she could have imagined the transaction. *"Un moment,"* he snapped, and got on his radio.

At that moment they heard a woman scream.

The security guard leaped forward and Kimi and Holden followed.

Following the scream, they raced into a scene of utter chaos. Simone, in her signature black, was on her knees. Her normally pale face was the color of sushi rice. In front of her stood a model who was rapidly falling into hysterics. Arianne Boucle, Simone's favorite, a dark-haired, dark-eyed beauty, six feet tall, was flapping her arms, hyperventilating and crying hysterically. She was also stark naked.

"Where's the dress?" Kimi demanded of the model.

She broke into a torrent of French, so fast Kimi could barely keep up. But the gist of it was that one of the perfect diamonds had come loose. She had to get out on the runway. Now. It was almost her cue. The wedding gowns were almost finished. She was to wear the grand finale gown.

Tears spilled over her spiky lashes as she cursed; then shouted for a cigarette.

Kimi grabbed her arm. "The dresser. Where's the dresser?"

"I told you. She had to fix the dress. But she's gone. Nobody can find her."

"When did she leave?"

A hysterical hiccup. "I don't know. Five minutes? Ten? Somebody better find my dress."

Then she jerked out of Kimi's grasp and dashed over to her makeup girl.

Kimi knelt beside the weeping designer. "Simone, you've got to pull yourself together." But it was hopeless.

The woman was sobbing as though she'd lost a child. *"C'est fini!"* she wailed. *"Tout fini!"*

"You'll need to go out there and talk, give us time to get the dress back."

But Simone was beyond reason.

The director was standing like a statue, watching the crisis. "Get them to slow down or something," Kimi ordered.

"Already did."

"How long have we got?"

"Five minutes tops."

"Okay. Stall. Do whatever you have to. Go out front and tell jokes if you need to."

He looked down at Simone. Shrugged. "I'll do what I can."

"Did you see the dresser leave with the gown?" Kimi asked.

"It's chaos back here. Maybe someone in makeup saw something."

Holden headed toward the exit.

She asked the director, "Which way to the seamstresses?"

She ran in the indicated direction. As she plunged into the dim recesses of the opera house she hoped she didn't run into Vladimir or Brewster. At another time she'd have worried about coming face-to-face with the famous phantom, but right now she'd take a masked, operatic ghost over a gun-wielding thug in a heartbeat.

She found the seamstresses tucked around the corner looking tired and frazzled, but, of course, no one had seen ApplePie's wedding dress. And they were so busy with last-minute repairs, they hadn't seen the dresser either.

She caught up to Holden. "She can't have left. We didn't

see her. Could she be hiding? What if we got people searching down here?"

Frustration was written all over his face. "I was so sure they'd get the dress out of here fast. But maybe you're—" At that moment they both saw a shadowy figure dart across the corridor. It was the drab dresser they'd seen talking to Vladimir on the day of the lingerie-shopping trip, and she was carrying a large bag.

"Stop!" Holden shouted, and started sprinting.

"*Arrêt!*" Kimi echoed. Not that she thought the woman hadn't stopped because she didn't understand the English word. With one scared glance at them the woman raced away.

Holden took off like a top sprinter.

She followed as best she could, hobbled by the damned shoes.

Kimi heard the throbbing roar as the engine of a van started up, and ran faster, so fast she was in danger of toppling onto her face.

But years of experience in high heels came to her aid and she managed to stay upright while running as fast as she could.

She rounded the corner to the exit—suspiciously empty of security—where both the dresser and Holden had disappeared seconds ahead of her.

The woman looked around. Her face was pale and perspiring, but her sturdy leather flats and panic were helping her move faster than Kimi would have believed possible. The van was backing toward her down the alley, the back doors already open. It was one of Simone's own vans, so would never have caused a raised eyebrow.

Holden was gaining on the woman, but there was no

way he could make it before she and the large bag clasped to her chest got to the van.

"Throw the bag," a voice yelled from the driver's open window.

Holden must have figured out the meaning of the words, for he tossed down his camera bag and tackled the dresser as she was about to throw the precious bag into the back of the open van. With a cry of surprise and shock, she fell to the pavement. The van screeched to a halt.

Kimi ran forward. The bag had rolled along the dirty sidewalk, coming to rest against a lamppost displaying a poster about couture week.

Before the van's driver door had even opened, Kimi picked up the bag and turned to run it back.

There was confusion and shouting behind her. She paused, bag in hand, knowing that if Holden was in trouble she'd have to stay. Simone might not get her moment of supreme glory, but she would get the dress back.

But she saw that Holden's buddies had made it in time. Two guys with badges and guns shouted to the driver of the van and the last thing she saw was the van driver raising his hands in the air.

Holden rose off the street and hauled the woman up with him. "Go!" he shouted in her direction. Kimi turned and kept running.

She did a reverse sprint and by the time she got back to Simone's side, she couldn't even speak. She tossed the dress over to Simone, who hadn't moved.

Simone looked at the bag and then at her.

"Go," Kimi panted. "Dress her yourself."

The woman's sharp face lit up as she opened the bag.

And suddenly the old Simone was back. Barking orders, removing the dress with tenderness.

"It's creased."

"No time to fix it."

The still-naked but once more perfectly made-up Arianne rushed forward, and in less than a minute looked the most radiant, most expensively dressed bride that Kimi had ever seen.

"You're a queen," Simone barked at the model. "The greatest actress in the world. Now go."

Arianne seemed to grow even taller and with a nod, stepped forward to the runway.

Kimi peeked out from behind the curtain, still trying to catch her breath, a vicious stitch still stabbing at her side. There had obviously been a bit of a long pause and she could see the model doing a final pose in the penultimate gown in Simone's collection. It was lovely, of course, a sheath of silvery-white satin, sleek as a blade, with a tiny bounce of a frivolous train at the bottom.

She gazed over the audience, sitting polite but anxious, waiting for the finale, for the gown that had been written about, speculated on, imagined but never yet seen. She noticed her father and Claudia, seated three back from the runway. With a sick stab of shock she saw Vladimir flanking her sister; the two were sharing a glance, as if to say, I wonder if we'll get something this great for our wedding.

She couldn't believe he was even here, and her skin crawled at the idea of Claudia and that psycho together. She grew even colder when she realized that the only way he could be sitting there acting lovey-dovey was if he knew that she and Holden would never reappear to tell their story.

Her eyes continued to scan the audience from her position behind the curtain and, inevitably, she spotted Brewster. The bald faced arrogance of the man astonished her. She wondered who the two had sent to the warehouse to do the dirty work of getting rid of her and Holden, for it was obvious that he hadn't any more idea of retiring from fashion than Vladimir had of not marrying into one of the most prestigious families in Italy. Brewster wouldn't get his hands dirty, of course.

She imagined she'd even rate a lovely farewell piece from him in his column. Had her body ever been found.

As the expectant hush built—for the grand finale—she watched Brewster. He looked so smug. The bastard had even dressed to match the wedding dress, she realized, wearing a long coat in black, with silver and diamond trim. In his case, she doubted the diamonds were real—any more than he was. His ferret eyes almost gleamed with excitement. He'd orchestrated stealing the dress and now he was on hand to report on the devastation with his trademark cruel wit.

Except that Brewster Peacock was about to get the shock of his life.

20

SHE WATCHED Peacock who was all but licking his chops. The music changed, and all eyes went to the runway and out floated Arianne. She stopped and posed like a queen.

There were gasps all through the opera house. Kimi didn't think Brewster gasped. She thought perhaps he squeaked like the panicked rat he was.

Arianne continued to parade in a wedding dress that had even this jaded audience awestruck. Kimi had seen a lot of couture in her time, but never anything to rival this gown. Only Simone would use flawless diamonds where other designers might use bugle beads. The bodice flashed and flamed with cool fire, like passion, while the silk and feathers of the skirt and train denoted softness, a new start perhaps.

She caught a glimpse of Nicole Pietra, and the world's most famous actress looked absolutely stunned. Then she burst into tears and started clapping like crazy, jumping to her feet as she did so.

Her husband-to-be was soon on his feet clapping as enthusiastically. She thought of the old saw about it being bad luck for the groom to see the dress before the wedding, and thought how much worse luck it would have been if he hadn't seen it, as had almost happened.

As wave after wave of couture enthusiasts rose and

added to the deafening applause, she noticed Brewster quietly—or as quietly as a man in that coat could—sidle to the nearest exit. But he didn't get far. Two men silently moved to flank him, a third bringing up the rear. They had law enforcement written all over them. Short hair, bland suits encasing hard bodies, tough faces.

There was barely a ripple as Brewster was led away, since all attention was focused on Simone's grand finale.

Never one to let a moment of high drama drag out, Simone already had the rest of the models wearing wedding gowns return, where they formed a group at the end of the runway, Simone was in the center like a small black bird among a flock of swans.

Kimi's attention reverted to her family. She wondered how Holden and his buddies planned to get Vladimir out of there without making a production of it. She didn't want Claudia or her father drawn into the embarrassment of the arrest. There was only one way to protect her family. She had to separate her father and sister from Claudia's fiancé.

And, she realized as she saw Vladimir's tough, impassive face glance to where Brewster had been, she had to do it now.

She tried to figure out how to get a message to her father or sister—cell phones were forbidden at Simone's shows and would be confiscated. Security was tighter here than at the U.N.

Vladimir didn't know yet that she and Holden had escaped, so he wouldn't be too panicked. He'd simply think that the dresser had somehow failed. She'd send a note to her father, she decided. But even as she turned away to find someone with paper and pen, in her peripheral vision, she saw Vladimir speaking earnestly to Claudia, who nodded, said something to her father and rose. Vladimir then put his arm around his fiancée and, even while the models were still onstage, they moved toward an exit. Her father appeared annoyed. He clearly thought it showed bad manners to leave before the show was finished. The Russian must have claimed illness or something.

Kimi's stomach clenched as she saw the pair of them arm in arm, heading not for the main exit where Brewster had been taken, but for a side door.

If he got Claudia out, unchecked…she didn't let herself finish the sentence, and moved quickly. From backstage she hurried in the direction she'd seen them leave.

She heard them before she saw them. Claudia's voice said, "Vladimir, you're going too fast."

"Need to get some air. Feel like I'm going to puke."

"The exit's the other way. Let me get you a medic."

"No."

Kimi came around the corner in time to see her father appear. Damn. "What is the problem?"

"Vladimir's sick. I think he's disoriented."

"Maybe if you could bring the car around," Vladimir said to her father. "I don't want to go back out there. I think I'm going to be sick."

"Don't go anywhere with him. He's not sick," Kimi said, rushing over to join the group.

When he saw her, Vladimir didn't gasp or shout out, but he did pale enough that indeed he looked sick.

"Kimi!" Claudia cried. "Where have you been?"

"It's a long story, but I was involved in trying to stop the theft of a couture piece." She looked at her sister and realized how delicate their new relationship was and that what she was about to say might destroy it forever. "I'm so sorry, Claudia. But Vladimir is part of a couture theft ring."

"What?" The big blue eyes so like her own widened. "Is this some kind of joke?"

"Of course it is," Vladimir said. "She must be on drugs or something."

"What proof do you have?" her father snapped.

She walked closer, to where the light was better and revealed her wrists. They were chafed red, and already bruises were beginning to show. "Vladimir and Brewster Peacock kidnapped Holden and me. They left us tied up and tried to steal Nicola Pietra's wedding gown." She was still speaking directly to Claudia, who tried to step forward when she saw the state of Kimi's wrists, but Vladimir held her tight, leaning his head on her shoulder and holding her in place. Claudia might see that as need but Kimi knew he was controlling her.

"Vladimir?"

"She's crazy. Trying to make trouble." He groaned loudly. "I feel really bad. Can you get the car? We can sort all this out tomorrow."

She and Giovanni exchanged a glance. "I'll get the car," he said. "Claudia? Why don't you come with me."

"No, Papa. I'll stay here."

"I'll return as quickly as I can."

Once more he looked at Kimi and then he walked swiftly away.

Her eyes closed briefly. This wasn't the time to think about betrayal. Her father barely knew her; of course the story would sound crazy.

Now she needed to convince Claudia not to go with Vladimir and hope like hell that somebody would come along who could separate the woman from her fiancé. She fingered the whistle around her neck, but Vladimir's grasp on Claudia made her cautious.

Instead, she tried to reason with her sister. "Please, Claudia. I would never try to hurt you."

"Nobody believes you," Vladimir sneered, glaring at her with his cold, cold eyes. "Why don't you go away."

"She's not going anywhere. I don't understand any of this, but Kimi needs a doctor too."

"You should step away from him, Claudia. He's a dangerous man."

"Come on, you've known her for two days. I'm going to be your husband. Who are you going to believe?"

She didn't move, but she said to Kimi, "Why would he do something like that?"

"For money. I don't know much about Vladimir's business, but I don't think most of it is legal."

"I don't have time for this," the Russian said. "I'm gonna puke. Come on."

He made a move for the back exit, pulling Claudia with him, but she stepped out from under his arm. "You go. I'll catch up."

His face turned ugly. "You're going to believe some American psycho over me? I'll leave you if you do."

Claudia's eyes filled with tears as she glanced from one to the other. Then she stepped closer to Kimi. "She's my sister."

"You're going to regret that decision." He reached into his jacket. Kimi hadn't imagined he could have a weapon on him, how had he got through security? What if she'd put Claudia in danger while trying to protect her?

"No!" she cried, even as the exit door behind them opened and Claudia's father's driver entered, followed closely by her father. And Holden.

She realized in that moment that her father's chauffeur was more than a driver. He came in with weapon drawn, a big man with steady eyes and a steady hand.

But Vladimir was a split second ahead of him. He grabbed Claudia with one hand, attempting to haul her against him while with the other drawing out a gun.

"No!" the sisters cried as one. Kimi held on to Claudia as she attempted to get free of Vladimir. Holden threw himself in front of the women.

The noise of a gun firing in the small space was deafening. For a second, Kimi wasn't sure who had fired, then she heard a string of Russian curses and, over Holden's shoulder, saw Vladimir on the ground. Her father grabbed the gun that had fallen to the floor.

"Are you okay?" Holden asked her.

"Yes."

"Claudia?"

The younger woman was trembling and her voice was barely audible. "Yes. Thank you."

The gunshot drew a small crowd, mostly security guys and cops. Kimi heard one of them call for paramedics.

Claudia stepped forward. Her hand shook as she yanked off the large diamond on her left hand.

"Vladimir, I am officially ending our engagement."

He groaned.

She tossed the engagement ring onto his chest where it

flashed in garish imitation of the diamonds on Simone's wedding dress.

Holden and the driver ushered Claudia, Kimi and Giovanni outside.

"My daughter," Giovanni said, folding Claudia into his arms. Then he turned. "And my other daughter." He turned to Kimi and embraced her as tenderly.

"I thought you didn't believe me," she said against his shoulder, which was broad and fatherly, feeling suddenly misty.

"Of course I did. I was trying to send you a signal that you were to stay with Claudia while I alerted the authorities."

"Oh."

"Now, I must take you to a doctor and have you checked out after being so mistreated by those animals."

Kimi shook her head. "I'm all right, really."

"Nonsense. I'm your father. You'll do what I say."

She bit back a smile. It was kind of nice to be ordered around by a father. Not that she had any intention of following his order.

"I'll take her, sir," Holden said.

There was a tiny pause. Her father nodded. "Be sure that you do. I will call on you tomorrow, Kimi, to make certain you are all right."

"Thank you."

He kissed her forehead.

"Good night, Kimi," Claudia said, then gave her a hug. "I'm sorry about Vladimir."

She nodded, and hugged tighter. Then they left and Claudia slid into the dark blue sedan whose door was being held open for her by the uniformed driver.

THEY WATCHED the Mercedes drive away, then she turned to Holden and simply walked into his arms. "We did it."

"Yes, we did."

She leaned up on her toes and nibbled his lips. "Now what shall we do?"

"Take you straight to a doctor."

"I don't need a doctor."

"I promised your father," he said.

"But—"

"Don't argue. If I don't have you checked out he'll have me taken out and horsewhipped."

Her lips curved. In her whole life she'd never had two such bossy men order her around. "You're not afraid of my father."

"Truth is, I want somebody to bandage my wrists, and I'll look like a pansy if I go alone."

She laughed. "I'm stuck between two strong-minded bullies."

He kissed her. "Get used to it. I don't think your father is going anywhere."

But you are, she thought sadly, as she called for her car.

While they were waiting, there was a small commotion, and then a nearly distraught Nicola Pietra dashed over to them and threw herself into Kimi's arms. *"Grazie,"* she cried. "Simone told us all. We almost lost our beautiful dress. You have saved my wedding. *Grazie.*"

"You're welcome," Kimi said. "I wish you every happiness."

Mark Apple followed more slowly. He shook Holden's hand solemnly. "Thanks, man."

21

"THAT WAS a couture week to remember," Kimi said the following night as she strolled with Holden beside the river, remembering another walk they'd taken by the river only a few days earlier.

"It was a week to remember in every way," he said, turning her to face him. He kissed her so very sweetly, and she thought how much she wanted to stay exactly like this, in this perfect moment, and not return to her neatly packed cases, and her early ride to the airport.

Holden had compromised on the hospital visit, having the on-site paramedics bandage Kimi's wrists. Naturally, she'd made them clean and bandage his as well. They both wore long sleeves tonight. She was in a black Armani dress and a string of pearls, so she felt she looked Italian, and demure enough that she had been certain of her father's approval when he and Claudia had come to bid her goodbye. Claudia was pale and it was obvious she'd been crying, but Kimi thought she saw enough strength and pride in her sister to know she'd be okay. The three had all shed a few tears at parting.

Now they were gone, and her time with Holden was down to hours.

"I wish we had more time," she said when at last he drew back, and she managed not to cling.

"Yeah. Me too."

"But," she said, forcing a smile, "I've got stories to file and work piling up in New York."

He nodded. "And I've got a business in Oregon."

"I know."

"Come back to my hotel for a bit. I've got something for you."

She should refuse, she knew that. There weren't many hours left until she had to be on that plane, but she figured she'd have years to sleep and not many hours left with Holden, so it was a no-brainer.

They walked back to his hotel and, once in his room, he handed her a gift-wrapped box. At first she thought it was clothing, but when she held it, the box was too heavy. More like a book.

He seemed a tiny bit nervous as she removed the wrapping. Inside, the box had the name of a photography studio here in Paris. She lifted open the box and saw that it was a photograph album. A beautiful one, in midnight-blue leather with a gold lock and key. On the cover he'd had printed the words One Night in Paris.

Using the tiny gold key, she unlocked the album and opened it.

"Oh, Holden," she said, feeling a rush of heat wash over her as she saw the first of the pictures he'd taken of her that magical night.

He came and sat beside her. "I wanted you to have something to remember our time together, and one of the most amazing nights I've ever spent."

She turned each page slowly, thinking how much artistry was in each photograph, and how much passion. She could feel the sexuality burning through the pages. Even though she was naked, or near-naked in many of the photos, it wasn't shame or embarrassment she felt but awe that Holden had seen and recorded her most intimate self. His feelings were expressed as though he'd spoken them aloud. She felt his pleasure in her body, the way he'd touched her with his photographer's eye told her everything she needed to know.

He loved her.

The last picture was the only one of the two of them in the album, and she thought it would be the one she turned to most in the days and weeks to come, when she thought back on this glorious time. The picture showed them in the Jardin des Tuileries pressed together, so their silhouettes seemed to merge in shadow. His body, strong and muscular, hers soft and supple, the statue looming over them and the darkness of trees around them.

She sat looking at that last photo for a long time. She felt him looking at her while she stared at the two of them in that intimate pose. She wished she had the words to express to him what he'd given her in these pages, but then, she thought he knew. "This is beautiful. The whole week—it's all been so…"

"I know." He kissed her and she felt the familiar rush of heat tempered with the sadness of knowing this was their last time together.

There were ways to say I love you that used no words. It was in the way he slid her zipper down slowly, kissing his way down her spine in its wake. It was in the way he eased the dress off her body and, instead of tossing it onto the floor, laid it on the chair because he understood clothes mattered to her.

She was wearing her favorite new bra-and-panties set, gossamer-thin black silk that was so sheer it was more like shadow than fabric.

"I love the way the light hits your breasts just here," he murmured, brushing the highlighted peaks. "And the shadows here," he said, kissing the valley between.

Emotion seemed to make her skin more sensitive, her blood pound faster.

She began undressing him, taking her own sweet time with buttons, treating herself to the emerging view of his muscular torso, while his hands touched her through lingerie, teasing them both.

When she got his jeans open she couldn't resist reaching down and wrapping her hand around his cock, enjoying all that heat and hardness so soon to be inside her.

As though following her lead, Holden slipped a hand into her panties and stroked her clit in rhythmic circles until she was boneless and light-headed. Even as she fell backward onto the bed on a cry of release, she kept her grip tight around him, tugging him with her so he fell on top of her.

He scrambled out of the rest of his clothes and she kicked off her heeled sandals, then he came to her and slipped her panties off. When he came back to her, she felt a lump form in her throat as he held her gaze, his eyes dark and serious while he entered her with quiet ceremony.

As their bodies moved together, as their mouths met, she

felt the absolute perfect happiness of this moment tinged with the sadness of knowing it would soon be gone.

When he cried out against her mouth, it sounded like a shout of protest.

AT FOUR she rose. The cab was coming at five, and with this flight she'd be in her office in time to put in most of a day's work.

When she got out of the shower, Holden passed her a cup of coffee.

"You should have gone back to sleep," she told him.

"Nah. I like to drag out my goodbyes."

She put on her stockings. "I wish it didn't have to be goodbye."

He shrugged. "It's not easy to keep up a relationship with so many miles between us, Manhattan."

"Come to New York," she said suddenly. "Come and let me show you my favorite restaurants. We can walk in Central Park and do the museums and see theater and ballet and opera."

He scratched his cheek and the sound of stubble rasping against his fingernails sounded ridiculously sexy to her. "Opera, huh?"

"See how the other half lives."

"Or you could come to Oregon. I can show you sights you've never seen in your life. We'll kayak with sea lions, cook the fish we catch over an open fire, watch the sun rise from the top of a mountain."

"Mountains, huh?"

He grinned at her, a little crookedly, and put his hands on her shoulders. "Or we kiss goodbye and know that we'll always remember one of the greatest weeks of our lives."

22

ONE OF THE GREATEST weeks of their lives, she thought as she fell back into the routine of her job, her apartment, her friends and her usual life. Paris had been the greatest week, not only because she'd met Holden and cracked an international crime ring, but also because she'd found her other family. At last.

She and Claudia e-mailed almost every day and talked on the phone every week or two.

She had a sister.

Today there'd been an e-mail waiting for her when she got to work. Dear Kimi, I am glad that you are no longer jet lagged. I feel as though I have terrible jet lag. Of course, it's only a broken engagement. I refuse to say heart. I am sure I never really loved that man. I intend to believe that, anyway, until it is true.

She sounded so down that Kimi wished she could do something for her.

Before she'd completed the next thought in her head, she pressed Reply. Dear Claudia, I have a fantastic idea. Come to New York. You'd love it here. I've got plenty of room and we could... Her fingers paused above the keyboard. They could what? They were two women from different worlds who barely knew each other. Did she really want her depressed Italian half sister as a houseguest?

Yes, she thought with a flicker of excitement. She did. We could shop, eat wonderful food and ignore all men. Think about it. She glanced at the clock on her computer. I have to go now, I'm having lunch with my mother. You must meet my mother, she's impossible to describe, but I think you'd like each other.

Normally, Kimi and her mom had dinner together every couple of weeks when they were both in town, it was a chance for two busy career women to catch up. But, after her Paris trip, they'd decided to fit in lunch as soon as they could.

"He's still handsome," her mother sighed over moo-shoo pork on Mott Street as she looked at the photos Kimi had brought of her father. "Claudia's a good-looking young woman too. Not as pretty as you, of course, but there's definitely a resemblance."

"I want you to meet her. I invited her to come to New York."

Her mother's brows rose. "You're not planning a parent trap, are you?"

Kimi laughed. "No, Mom. I can't even imagine you and Giovanni together. Not even when you were young. How did you two ever get together in the first place?"

"Sex. Of course."

Kimi rolled her eyes. "I figured that part out, thanks. But, in a campus crawling with guys in Birkenstocks quoting Emily Dickinson, how did you end up with an Italian business major?"

Her mother pushed her gray-and-black hair over her shoulder. She was, as she liked to tell Kimi, aging gracefully, but the silver-and-black threads in her hair were stunning and it was a look that people were currently paying a fortune for in New York salons.

At fifty her mom remained beautiful in an earth-mother way. And, though she'd sworn she'd never marry, Kimi knew that Evelyn's toothbrush was rarely the only one residing in her bathroom. Currently, the guy with the wooden-handled, hemp-bristled toothbrush was a philosophy professor named Bryant. Kimi thought he was a pompous windbag, but her mom said he was great in bed and had an unexpectedly quirky sense of humor. Whatever.

She could almost see her mom sifting back through the years and her various lovers to reconnect with those few months almost thirty years ago.

"I suppose the simple truth was, not that opposites attract, which is patently ridiculous, but that sometimes we have a powerful sexual attraction to someone with whom we have no other possible way of connecting." She shrugged and the shisha mirrors woven into her jacket—hand-crafted by fair-trade female artisans in India—flashed. "I can't explain it. Hasn't that ever happened to you?"

Kimi sat back and regarded her mother. "I think it just did."

"Oh, good. Tell me all the delicious details."

"You know, you're more like a girlfriend than a mother."

A wicked grin answered her. "I tried my best to be a good mother, but I have to say it was a relief when you grew up and I could relax and enjoy you as a friend."

Kimi laughed. It was true. They loved each other, but they did a lot better now that they didn't share a roof. "I guess you and I are a perfect example of people who love each other but have nothing in common."

"But I never loved Giovanni. Anyway, that's old history. Tell me about your wildly inappropriate lover." She slipped a snow pea into her mouth. "In Paris of course?"

She nodded. "His name's Holden and he's a private investigator. We worked together—well, I guess I helped him do his job, and we busted a couture theft ring, which you already know."

Her mother was watching her carefully. Not much got past her. "And?"

"And it was fantastic," she wailed. "But he lives in Oregon and he's an outdoors guy. You know, hiking boots and lumberjack shirts."

Her mother's lips twitched. "No designer suits and Italian loafers?"

"His designer is Eddie Bauer. His hobby is photographing wildlife." She leaned in and dropped her voice as though relating a dirty secret. "He camps. In a tent."

Her mother hooted with laughter. "All those years I tried to instill in you other values than which skirt went with which top, in which pursuit I failed mightily, and you fall in love with Jeremiah Johnson. Oh, it's delicious."

She groaned. Not even bothering to deny she was in love with the guy. Trust her mother to home in on the pertinent detail. "What am I going to do?"

"You've got two choices. Forget about him or track him down like the rare and endangered species he is."

"What are you saying? A good man is hard to find?"

"No. I'm saying that a man who doesn't dress prettier than I do is going to make me—and you—a lot happier than those useless twits you usually go for."

A waiter came over with a fresh pot of green tea. Even in the most crowded restaurants in Manhattan her mother always got better service than anyone she knew.

"I swore after my last summer boot camp for paramili-

tary feminists in training that I was never going to put on
a pair of hiking boots again."

Her mother poured the tea. "It was summer camp to
build self-esteem and survival skills. Don't exaggerate.
And, like I said, you have a choice."

"Yeah… But it doesn't feel like much of a choice. I can't
stop thinking about him." Or paging through the album
he'd made her. When she got to the last page, she noticed,
not their obvious differences, but how well they blended
together in the most basic way of all.

Her mother leaned over and patted her shoulder.
"Maybe there's an Eddie Bauer on Fifth Avenue."

She groaned and put her head in her hands.

"I'm joking, Kimi."

"I passed an outdoors store on the way here. I almost
told the cab to stop. That's how pathetic I am."

A low laugh and sparkling excitement in her mom's
eyes told Kimi that Evelyn was enjoying this much more
than a good mother ought to. "Then you can find it on
your way back. I don't have to work this afternoon. I'll
come with you."

"That's ridiculous. I'm not going in."

She was still arguing when the cab dropped them
outside the store. There was a yellow mountaineer's pack
in the window, an ice ax and red rope. Ridiculous.

She followed her mother inside. The place even smelled
like tent when she walked in, and of all the sensory recol-
lections stored in her memory bank that evoked strong reactions, the smell of tent was right up there with puke.

She edged to the door, thinking this was not her place
and these were not her people, when a young girl wearing

a Team Everest T-shirt and a nose ring came up and asked if they needed any help.

Her mother, for once, didn't open her mouth. Clearly, she knew that it was up to Kimi now.

The salesclerk wore her blond hair in a ponytail, no makeup but clear lip gloss, cargo pants and sneakers. She had the bright eyes and glowing complexion of an outdoors buff, and muscular arms and legs. This was the sort of woman for Holden, not a designer-obsessed fashionista.

But she'd come this far. She flashed a smile at the young woman and said, "I haven't worn a pair of hiking boots in more than ten years." She glanced at her companion. "My mom made me go to these awful wilderness camps for girls—"

"Wow, cool."

"Not for me. Anyhow, I was thinking I should give the outdoors another try."

"You totally should. You know, boots are a lot lighter and technically enhanced than they used to be."

Oh, great. Technically enhanced hiking boots. Just what she needed. "Look, the truth is, I met a guy. He's the outdoors type. I wanted to see if I could stand it, maybe for a weekend."

The blonde looked her up and down. She was wearing a Dior pencil skirt, an Emilio Pucci blouse from last season, cherry colored Kate Spade bag and Prada open-toed sandals. "He must be some guy."

She grinned. "Oh, he is."

"Okay. Let's start with the boots. Your number-one most important piece of hiking equipment. Where will you be hiking?"

She tossed a helpless glance at her mother, who said, "Oregon."

"Okay. You'll need rain gear."

"Rain gear." Forty minutes later, there was a four-hundred-dollar charge on her card and she owned gray hiking boots, a guaranteed-to-stay-dry-in-all-weather jacket and assorted hiking garb. For four hundred bucks she could have had two Hermès scarves, the Dior sunglasses she'd seen in Saks yesterday, a pair of—no! She had to stop.

She was doing this. Holden had already proved he could play in her world. Maybe it was time to see if she could play in his.

After leaving her mother, she returned to her office and wondered if she should have called Holden first before her little shopping spree. They hadn't spoken since they got back to the States. There was no point in dragging out the inevitable, but she was beginning to wonder if parting was inevitable.

She thought of the photograph album she kept on her bedside table so it was the last thing she saw at night and the first thing she noticed in the morning. Maybe love was stronger than their differences.

Or maybe not. There was only one way to find out.

She called his cell phone. "MacGreggor."

And hearing him say his last name had her knowing she was doing the right thing. If his voice uttering one word could make her almost woozy, she couldn't imagine what Holden in the flesh could do in a weekend. She shut her eyes briefly. Even if Holden and his flesh were in a tent.

"Holden, it's me, Kimi."

There was a tiny pause. Delighted surprise, she hoped.

"Kimi. Hi. Where are you?"

"I'm in my office. But I've got an assignment in Seattle."

"That's great, when?"

"The timing's flexible," especially since she didn't actually have an assignment in Seattle and she'd be scrambling to put one together if this worked out. "I thought I'd take a few extra days and come visit you."

"Visit me."

She looked at the bag of outdoors stuff that she could swear still smelled faintly of tent. "I was hoping to take you up on your offer to go, um, camping."

He chuckled. "Seriously?"

"Why not? You made those sunrises sound pretty good."

"It is so great to hear your voice." He dropped his to a soft murmur. "I missed you."

She smiled into the phone. "Me too."

"Figure out your timing and I'll clear my schedule. How much time can you give me?"

"I don't know. A few days."

"Five. I'll need five days to take you where I want you to go."

She swallowed. "Five days in a tent?"

She could almost hear his grin. "No. Five nights in a tent. The days we'll go out." He dropped his voice. "Unless we decide to stay in bed."

Beneath the horror of what she'd committed to, Kimi experienced the excitement of knowing she was going to have him all to herself for five days and nights.

THE MINUTE SHE SAW him again, all her anxieties, second thoughts and exasperated *this is not me* visions of herself disappeared. Holden was there, at the airport, to meet her, folding her into his arms so tightly she thought she might spend the next five days in a hospital instead of a tent.

Eventually, he drew back and she saw the man she'd first seen. A little rumpled, rough and outdoorsy. And he looked better to her than the whole fall Armani collection put together.

His eyes crinkled as he took a good look at her. "You're wearing hiking boots."

"Don't gloat."

"I'm not. You look fantastic."

She leaned in close. "Under all this outdoors gear I am wearing silk lingerie from Paris."

In the middle of the airport he threw back his head and laughed. "You are definitely my ideal woman."

He grabbed her yellow backpack and hoisted it over his shoulder. "Let's go."

It didn't rain. Even though she brought the all-weather jacket, the weather was gorgeous for June. Warm and sunny. Her hiking boots were comfortable— of course she'd made a fool of herself breaking them in tramping through Central Park, but it was worth the trouble she'd taken. They were comfortable and sturdy and of course five days alone in a tent with Holden was an entirely different experience than a month in tents packed with teenage girls—apart from the three terrifying days and nights she'd been completely alone in the wilderness.

"You have to admit the great outdoors has some advantages over a crowded city," Holden murmured in her ear on their fourth day. They were both naked. Sunlight dappled their skin and only the trees and the odd chipmunk were around to witness their passion.

"You think this view is better than the Eiffel Tower?"

He nuzzled her breast. "Definitely."

Tomorrow they'd drive back to his place and then she'd fly out the next day, back home. Saying goodbye again.

Was this just another quick intense visit? Could they keep this up? A Steller's jay hopped to a nearby rock and perched there, its head to one side, blue wings ready for flight, observing them greedily, hoping for handouts. To her amusement, she was starting to know the local flora and fauna, thanks to her mountain-man tour guide.

She rested her head on his chest, listening to the steady thump of his heart. "You know," she said, "I've been thinking."

"Mmm. Me too."

"Really? What about?"

"How well you fit in with my life. Once you quit whining about missing macchiatos and your eyelash curler, you did okay."

She smacked him. "The only thing I whined about was my cell phone. I've never been this far from a phone since the cell phone was commercially available."

"There's no service up here. No point in lugging a cell around. Only a global phone works out here." He brushed his palm over her breast and she shivered. "You did good."

"I'm having fun. You have possibly cured me of the outdoor-experience phobia I developed in wilderness-survival camp."

"Was it watching the pod of orcas that convinced you?"

"No. Spectacular as that was, I think it was all the great sex that sold me."

He chuckled, then suddenly grew serious, and with an expression in his eyes that made her pulse quicken, he kissed her, the kind of kiss that says more than words can. But then he said the words anyway. "I love you."

A weird noise, almost like a ringing phone interrupted him. She raised her head. "What is that noise?"

"My global phone."

Her jaw dropped. "You have a global phone and you never told me?"

He didn't bother to answer the obvious, just jogged over to his pack—and she hoped he hurt his bare feet on the rocks—and hauled out the phone. "MacGreggor."

While she watched him on the phone he'd snuck in under her nose, he nodded. "Yeah, sure I'll hold."

He put his hand over the phone and said to her, "It's for emergencies only."

"What's the emergency?"

"I don't know yet." Then he held up a hand. "Hi. Uh, huh. Maybe." He shot her a look. "I might be interested." Then his lips quirked as though at a private joke. "Actually, yeah, I do know where Kimberley Renton is."

What? She mouthed. He waved her silent.

"I'll get her a message. Right. No, I understand. Absolutely. We'll get back to you."

She sat up. "What's going on? Who were you on the phone to? Why did my name come up?"

She made room for him on the blanket as he sat beside her. Their bare arms brushed and she was almost shocked by the warmth of his skin.

"I'll tell you in a minute, but first I want to finish what I was trying to say." He glared at where the phone was safely tucked away out of sight. "That's why I hate bringing a phone out here. I didn't want to be interrupted. The thing is, I thought we were going back to our completely different lives. But I can't do that. I can't let you go."

"I know. Oh, Holden, I love you so much."

He opened his arms to her and folded her in tight.

"I did better than I thought I would here, but the thing is I'll always be Manhattan."

"I know. And I'll always be the outdoors guy."

"So?"

"So, we compromise. Spend time in each other's worlds. Maybe someday we'll find a place we both love."

"But what about our work. What about—"

The jay, obviously realizing that the two naked people weren't doing anything that involved food, flew off with an annoyed squawk.

"That call? It was ApplePie's PR firm."

"Why would they call you?"

He was grinning down at her. "Because Nicola Pietra and Mark Apple have decided to let two hand-selected members of the media in to photograph their wedding. It's a secret location, top-secret everything to keep out the paparazzi. They were so grateful to us for saving the dress and, they said that since they were going to put us on the invitation list anyway, we should be the ones to do the pictures and write the article."

She jumped to her feet and whooped, feeling the breeze soft against her skin and the bumpiness of the ground beneath the blanket.

"Do you know what this means? It's huge."

"I know. We can work together. I can get used to Manhattan. You can get used to Oregon. We'll work it out."

"We'll work it out," she agreed, so full of happiness she wanted to do something crazy. Skydive. Climb a mountain. Spend another five days in a tent. "And if we ever can't agree?"

He took her hand and kissed it. "We'll meet in Paris."

* * * * *

*Look for LAST WOLF WATCHING
by Rhyannon Byrd—the exciting conclusion
in the BLOODRUNNERS miniseries
from Silhouette Nocturne.*

*Follow Michaela and Brody on their fierce journey
to find the truth and face the demons from the past,
as they reach the heart of the battle between
the Runners and the rogues.*

*Here is a sneak preview of book three,
LAST WOLF WATCHING.*

Michaela squinted, struggling to see through the impenetrable darkness. Everyone looked toward the Elders, but she knew Brody Carter still watched her. Michaela could feel the power of his gaze. Its heat. Its strength. And something that felt strangely like anger, though he had no reason to have any emotion toward her. Strangers from different worlds, brought together beneath the heavy silver moon on a night made for hell itself. That was their only connection.

The second she finished that thought, she knew it was a lie. But she couldn't deal with it now. Not tonight. Not when her whole world balanced on the edge of destruction.

Willing her backbone to keep her upright, Michaela Doucet focused on the towering blaze of a roaring bonfire that rose from the far side of the clearing, its orange flames burning with maniacal zeal against the inky black curtain

of the night. Many of the Lycans had already shifted into
their preternatural shapes, their fur-covered bodies
standing like monstrous shadows at the edges of the forest
as they waited with restless expectancy for her brother.

Her nineteen-year-old brother, Max, had been attacked
by a rogue werewolf—a Lycan who preyed upon humans
for food. Max had been bitten in the attack, which meant
he was no longer human, but a breed of creature that
existed between the two worlds of man and beast, much
like the Bloodrunners themselves.

The Elders parted, and two hulking shapes emerged from
the trees. In their wolf forms, the Lycans stood over seven
feet tall, their legs bent at an odd angle as they stalked
forward. They each held a thick chain that had been wound
around their inside wrists, the twin lengths leading back into
the shadows. The Lycans had taken no more than a few steps
when they jerked on the chains, and her brother appeared.

Bound like an animal.

Biting at her trembling lower lip, she glanced left, then
right, surprised to see that others had joined her. Now the
Bloodrunners and their family and friends stood as a united
force against the Silvercrest pack, which had yet to accept
the fact that something sinister was eating away at its foun-
dation—something that would rip down the protective
walls that separated their world from the humans'. It
occurred to Michaela that loyalties were being announced
tonight—a separation made between those who would
stand with the Runners in their fight against the rogues and
those who blindly supported the pack's refusal to face
reality. But all she could focus on was her brother. Max
looked so hurt...so terrified.

"Leave him alone," she screamed, her soft-soled, black satin slip-ons struggling for purchase in the damp earth as she rushed toward Max, only to find herself lifted off the ground when a hard, heavily muscled arm clamped around her waist from behind, pulling her clear off her feet. "Damn it, let me down!" she snarled, unable to take her eyes off her brother as the golden-eyed Lycan kicked him.

Mindless with heartache and rage, Michaela clawed at the arm holding her, kicking her heels against whatever part of her captor's legs she could reach. "Stop it," a deep, husky voice grunted in her ear. "You're not helping him by losing it. I give you my word he'll survive the ceremony, but you have to keep it together."

"Nooooo!" she screamed, too hysterical to listen to reason. "You're monsters! All of you! Look what you've done to him! How dare you! *How dare you!*"

The arm tightened with a powerful flex of muscle, cinching her waist. Her breath sucked in on a sharp, wailing gasp.

"Shut up before you get both yourself and your brother killed. I will *not* let that happen. Do you understand me?" her captor growled, shaking her so hard that her teeth clicked together. "Do you understand me, Doucet?"

"Damn it," she cried, stricken as she watched one of the guards grab Max by his hair. Around them Lycans huffed and growled as they watched the spectacle, while others outright howled for the show to begin.

"That's enough!" the voice seethed in her ear. "They'll tear you apart before you even reach him, and I'll be damned if I'm going to stand here and watch you die."

Suddenly, through the haze of fear and agony and

outrage in her mind, she finally recognized who'd caught her. *Brody.*

He held her in his arms, her body locked against his powerful form, her back to the burning heat of his chest. A low, keening sound of anguish tore through her, and her head dropped forward as hoarse sobs of pain ripped from her throat. "Let me go. I have to help him. *Please*," she begged brokenly, knowing only that she needed to get to Max. "Let me go, Brody."

He muttered something against her hair, his breath warm against her scalp, and Michaela could have sworn it was a single word…. But she must have heard wrong. She was too upset. Too furious. Too terrified. She must be out of her mind.

Because it sounded as if he'd quietly snarled the word *never*.

nocturne™

THE FINAL INSTALLMENT OF
THE BLOODRUNNERS TRILOGY

Last Wolf Watching

Runner Brody Carter has found his match in
Michaela Doucet, a human with unusual psychic powers.
When Michaela's brother is threatened, Brody becomes
her protector, and suddenly not only has to protect her
from her enemies but also from himself....

LOOK FOR
LAST WOLF WATCHING
BY
RHYANNON BYRD

Available May 2008 wherever you buy books.

Dramatic and Sensual Tales of Paranormal Romance

www.eHarlequin.com   SN61786

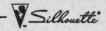

SPECIAL EDITION™

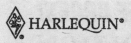

HARLEQUIN®

American ★ Romance®

Three Boys and a Baby

When Ella Garvey's eight-year-old twins and
their best friend, Dillon, discover an abandoned
baby girl, they fear she will be put in jail—
or worse! They decide to take matters into their
own hands and run away. Luckily the outlaws are
found quickly…and Ella finds a second chance
at love—with Dillon's dad, Jackson.

LOOK FOR

Three Boys and a Baby

BY

LAURA MARIE ALTOM

*Available May
wherever you buy books.*

LOVE, HOME & HAPPINESS

REQUEST YOUR FREE BOOKS!

2 FREE NOVELS PLUS 2 FREE GIFTS!

HARLEQUIN®

Blaze™

Red-hot reads!

HARLEQUIN *Romance*

Western Weddings

Jason Welborn was convinced that his business
partner's daughter, Jenny, had come to claim her share
in the business. But Jenny seemed determined to win
him over, and the more he tried to push her away, the
more feisty Jenny's response. Slowly but surely she
was starting to get under Jason's skin....

Look for

Coming Home to the Cattleman

by

JUDY CHRISTENBERRY

Available May wherever you buy books.

HARLEQUIN®
Live the emotion™

www.eHarlequin.com

HRI7511

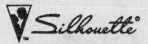

Silhouette®

Romantic
SUSPENSE

Sparked by Danger,
Fueled by Passion.

Seduction Summer:
Seduction in the sand…and a killer on the beach.

Silhouette Romantic Suspense invites you to the hottest
summer yet with three connected stories from some
of our steamiest storytellers! Get ready for…

Killer Temptation
by Nina Bruhns;
a millionaire this tempting is worth a little danger.

Killer Passion
by Sheri WhiteFeather;
an FBI profiler's forbidden passion incites a
killer's rage,

and

Killer Affair
by Cindy Dees;
this affair with a mystery man is to die for.

Look for

KILLER TEMPTATION by Nina Bruhns in June 2008
KILLER PASSION by Sheri WhiteFeather in July 2008
and
KILLER AFFAIR by Cindy Dees in August 2008.

Available wherever you buy books!

Visit Silhouette Books at www.eHarlequin.com   SRS27586

COMING NEXT MONTH

#393 INDULGE ME Isabel Sharpe
Forbidden Fantasies

Darcy Wolf has three wild fantasies she's going to fulfill before she leaves town. But after seducing her hottie housepainter Tyler Houston, she might just have to put Fantasy #2 and Fantasy #3 on hold!

#394 NIGHTCAP Kathleen O'Reilly
Those Sexy O'Sullivans, Bk. 3

Sean O'Sullivan—watch out! Three former college girlfriends have just hatched a revenge plot on the world's most lovable womanizer. Cleo Hollings, in particular, is anxious to get started on her make-life-difficult-for-Sean plan. Only, she never guesses how difficult it will be for her when she starts sleeping with the enemy.

#395 UP CLOSE AND PERSONAL Joanne Rock

Who's impersonating sizzling sensuality guru Jessica Winslow? Rocco Easton is going undercover to find out. And he has to do it soon, because the identity thief is getting braver, pretending to be Jessica everywhere—even in his bed!

#396 A SEXY TIME OF IT Cara Summers
Extreme

Bookstore owner Neely Rafferty can't believe it when she realizes that the time-traveling she does in her dreams is actually real. And so, she soon discovers, is the sexy time-cop who's come to stop her. Max Gale arrives in 2008 with a job to do. And he'll do it, too—if Neely ever lets him out of her bed....

#397 FIRE IN THE BLOOD Kelley St. John
The Sexth Sense, Bk. 4

Chantalle Bedeau is being haunted by a particularly nasty ghost, and the only person who can help her is medium Tristan Vicknair. Sure, she hasn't seen him since their incredible one-night stand but what's the worst he can do—give her the best sex of her life again?

#398 HAVE MERCY Jo Leigh
Do Not Disturb

Pet concierge Mercy Jones has seen it all working at the exclusive Hush Hotel in Manhattan. But when sexy Will Desmond saunters in with his pooch she's shocked by the fantasies he generates. This is one man who could unleash the animal in Mercy!

HBCNM0408